IT'S ALWAYS A PUSSYCAT
a singer's approach to choral conducting

Edward Caswell

LINDSAY MUSIC

First published by Lindsay Music 2017

Lindsay Music
24 Royston Street, Potton, Bedfordshire,
SG19 2LP, UK

www.lindsaymusic.co.uk

© Lindsay Music 2017

Edward Caswell has asserted his right under the Copyright, Patents and Designs Act 1988 to be identified as author of this work.

Cover design
Leporello Uitgevers NL - Geert Gratama

ALL RIGHTS RESERVED.

No part of this publication may be reproduced or transmitted in any form or by any means, electronic or mechanical, including photocopying, recording, or any information storage or retrieval system, or online without prior permission in writing from the publishers.

ISBN 0 85957 169 6

To Clare and Tali

"These days, where there is so much strife, so much war, so much destruction, to do something which is civilised in intent and I hope in result, at the top end of what is possible in a civilisation, what a privilege eh? What a privilege!"

Sir Peter Maxwell Davies CBE (1934-2016)

About the author

photograph courtesy of Renske Vrolijk

Since the 1980s Edward Caswell has been associated with many of Europe's finest choirs as singer, chorus master and conductor in music from every period and in every genre.

He works in Germany, The Netherlands and Belgium and lives in the Scottish Highlands where he founded Cromarty Youth Opera in 2013.

Contents

	Introduction	xi
1.	Getting the best out of your voice and everyone else's	1
2.	Warming up	2
3.	Rehearsing *The Evening Primrose* by Benjamin Britten	13
4.	Tips for rehearsing Handel's *Messiah*	23
5.	Tips for rehearsing Fauré's *Requiem*	27
6.	Tips for rehearsing Mozart's *Requiem*	29
7.	Tips for rehearsing Beethoven *Symphony No. 9* Finale	32
8.	Tips for rehearsing Verdi's *Requiem*	37
9.	Tips for rehearsing Brahms's *Ein deutsches Requiem*	44
10.	Tips for rehearsing Mendelssohn's *Elijah*	50
11.	Not conducting *O clap your hands* by Orlando Gibbons	54
12.	Rehearsing *At the Round Earth's Imagined Corners* by C. Hubert H. Parry	81
13.	Amen, Alleluja!	95

The works by Britten, Gibbons and Parry appear in full at the end of each relevant chapter

Introduction

However much I have identified myself as a choral director over the years, many of the singers in choirs I have worked with see me as a singing teacher, and often the only singing teacher they have ever had. I frequently teach people individually who have already sung in a choir I have taken, and I always start by telling them that they won't be hearing anything they haven't heard from me already. Of course there are benefits in the individual attention that can be given in a lesson, but the means of getting the very best out of the human voice should not remain the secrets of the one-to-one relationship. Ideally this knowledge will be at the heart of every choral rehearsal, so it makes sense for the choral director to think of himself or herself as having a lot in common with a singing teacher. For any number of reasons all manner of people end up taking choirs and they won't all come from a singing background. But a basic understanding of singing will improve the results they can achieve immeasurably. And here's some wonderful news: that basic understanding can be easily learned and put into practice, transforming the job that can be done with any choir, multiplying its expressive possibilities and enhancing the enjoyment and satisfaction of its members and eventually its audience. Really? Really! And this is a book for those who are starting from scratch, for those who are experienced but want to be able to do the job better, and indeed, for anyone open to new ideas about what we do.

1

Getting the best out of your voice and everybody else's

The idea of learning to sing or being taught to sing first entered my head when I was about seven years old. With other young choristers I was showing a guest around behind the scenes at St Peter's Bournemouth where my brother and I were in the choir. The training we received there was excellent, and the choir maintained a busy schedule with a wide and varied repertoire much of which I can still remember. When we reached our rehearsal room I remember hearing the question "And this is where you learn to sing?". And I distinctly remember thinking we're not actually taught to sing; we're just taught the music and we sing it. We were of course given a few tips but they didn't amount to much, and none of them has stuck in my mind the way the music from that period has.

As for many colleagues, the choral experience from the age of seven to my early twenties amounted to the musical training which would be the basis for how I would earn my living. Of course I had some singing lessons during this period, but only really in my preparation for auditioning for a postgraduate place at The Royal College of Music did I start to develop an idea of singing technique; how to get the best out of the voice. And once at the RCM I started to learn about singing; only started, because it took years. What took even longer was formulating a simple way to pass on this learning; a way that would make sense and be beneficial for singers of all ages and in all types of choir: from six year olds to people in their seventies, from community choirs to professional choirs. In all of these contexts in one sense the job is the same: getting the best sound out of the people in front of you. More surprising, particularly to the non-professional end of the spectrum, is the fact that the means of doing this varies very little. The handful of ideas that transform a community choir's rendition of the simplest song into something special and moving is the same handful of ideas that can transform a passage from an oratorio or opera sung by rows of professionals. Of course a community choir will never sing Beethoven's *Missa Solemnis* or the Verdi *Requiem*, there's a whole universe between them in that sense; but when it comes to getting a great sound, a sound the singers feel they are making with their whole bodies, a sound that connects with the audience communicating something memorable and moving, the same ideas are what the choral leader needs at his or her disposal. This knowledge and understanding is the distillation of years of training and years of experience as a singer, distilled so that it can be passed on easily, and quickly, and remembered, and referred to at any time so that a challenge can be overcome. In a rehearsal with a professional choir I was once asked a question about a high, loud bass entry: "Is it still a pussycat?". The answer came as no surprise to many of the choir who were used to my methods. "It's always a pussycat."

2

Warming up

Singing is a physical activity and like any other physical activity, a few exercises make a world of difference to how we perform, and what shape we will be in when we've finished. The warm-up also happens to be the exposition of the basic principles of singing.

From week to week, month to month, year to year, the warm-up will change a little. But it's important to remember that the fundamentals of singing, the handful of ideas, don't change at all, and therefore the warm-up shouldn't change very much. It's not a party game. I'm happy for it to have almost a feeling of ritual. It doesn't need to be solemn but a feeling of reassuring ritual can make it the ideal preparation for voice, body and mind.

Posture
Stand tall. It's probably the tallest you have been all day and you immediately feel different. Your chest is lifted and that's where it's going to stay. Think of the head as a helium-filled balloon, gently encouraging you to stand to your full height. Now, in order to loosen up a little, roll your shoulders, forwards a few times then backwards. Don't involve your head in this, it stays where it is, as your chest does.

Now start breathing through your nose. I sometimes refer to this as the Chanel No 5 moment, because if anyone is wearing it you will smell it now; two minutes of good posture and your tubes seem to be more open than they were. Your whole body feels different and better. Already!

Breathing
I remember hearing a very well established teacher at The Royal College of Music saying that once the breathing is sorted out most of the rest will fall into place. It didn't reassure me. In fact, it made me think that the breathing must therefore be very difficult to sort out. Oh dear! So much time and money is wasted on this simple matter, and understanding of this simple mechanism is so befogged by confusion. I sometimes ask people why we breathe when we sing; I've had some astonishing answers. We breathe when we sing for the simple reason that we would die if we didn't, and our breathing when singing is essentially the same breathing we are doing the rest of the time, while we're talking, while we're walking and while we're sleeping. And if the posture is right then with just a little help and explanation, the breathing will fall into place.

Let's get rid of a popular misconception. The man in the lift is wrong. How many times have you been in a crowded lift and heard someone say "Breathe in!"? It even happens to me on the way to rehearsals. Breathing in makes you bigger not smaller. What he wants you to do is pull everything in, principally your tummy, but that isn't breathing in. If you fill something flexible with a fluid it gets bigger. There can't be any argument about that.

So, with the posture we've learned I want you to pull your tummy in and let it go, and again. Keep repeating this and gradually get quicker. I call this belly-dancing. It's down here that we feel the expansion when we breathe in, not in the lungs. Of course it's the lungs which fill with air but they push everything else down and actually the feeling that the breath is coming from so low in our bodies can start to provide us with a real sense of being grounded while singing. Occasionally I am asked whether this is called abdominal breathing. It might be by some people but the term is nonsense to me. The air is in the lungs; air in the abdomen cannot be used for breathing!

Having established the flexibility of the belly-dancing muscles and effectively woken them up, we need to coordinate that flexibility with the breathing. So start puffing, slowly at first, letting the belly-dancing muscles go between each puff; then increase the speed of the puffs. Don't purse your lips tightly, rather, hold them just as you would if you were blowing out a candle. Tightly pursed lips create breath resistance inappropriate for a singing exercise. There is relatively little resistance to the breath when we sing, relative that is to playing a wind instrument in particular the oboe where the breath is pushed through a tiny opening in the lips under great pressure. During this exercise make sure you stay tall, that the chest is still lifted and that the shoulders haven't got involved.

This isn't the whole story of course, but it's a good start and we can deal with other aspects of the breathing when we start singing. I call the puffing exercise The Railway Children. I start it, the choir join in and gradually I get faster. Initially people find it hard to do quickly but that soon changes after practising it daily for a few minutes.

Humming

As a singer you need to be able to make high sounds, low sounds and mid-range sounds and get from one to the other instantly and easily; you need total flexibility through the range and we address this with a pitch-flexibility exercise.

Start humming in a completely random way: mid-range, high, low, high again. The likelihood is that you will tend to follow the pitch with your eyes, your eyebrows, your head or even your upper body. You need to stay still, in the position that will feel more and more comfortable after the work we have done on posture. So, only the pitch goes up and down.

There is more than one way to hum so let's make sure we're doing it right. Any sense of pushing, compression or focus is to be avoided however reassuring it may feel. You don't want to be pushing when you're singing and your humming is in some respects the basis of your singing. It needs to be free and not under pressure from any direction. This will make it less loud and you may feel that you have less control over it. You have. But learning to sing is about relinquishing the wrong kind of control; it's about letting it happen rather than making it happen, an idea I also like to apply to choral conducting when I'm tempted to try too hard!

We now need to impose some order on this random, free, beautiful thing. But not too much order. The basis of a flexible voice, even the most extraordinary *coloratura* singing, is the flexibility you are now just discovering; so it's crucial that as you now start to sing recognisable shapes they stay connected to that free feeling.

Before we start a simple exercise I need to warn you of two ever-present false friends. The first is the keyboard instrument. It's a machine constructed to produce individual pitches. It does this admirably and has done for centuries. But we've been singing for much longer! You are not a machine constructed to produce separate pitches and you need to resist the temptation to try to be. Time and time again I've seen a singer so disappointed by his or her attempt to reproduce an *arpeggio* played on the piano, that he or she stops halfway and apologises. The singer has tried to imitate something of an entirely different species and I shouldn't actually have played it. What the keyboard can't do is get between the pitches and this is what the singer is doing all the time. I remember hearing Dame Janet Baker say to students at The Royal College of Music that if you're singing this note followed by that note you should be singing every microtone in between. And listen to Luciano Pavarotti singing Puccini; that's what he's doing. How can this have any relevance to what we are trying to do with singers in a choir? These are great singers and however far removed your choir's repertoire might be from *La Bohème* we are identifying something that all singers should have in common. The other false friend is notation. You will realise this if you've listened to a Puccini opera with the score, particularly if you have come from the sort of church music background that I have. How separate the notes look, but how unseparately they are being treated by these extraordinary singers, and how right it sounds!

So let's hum a "messy scale", see figure 1, starting on A flat and going up by semitones. As you get higher you might find it easier to hum on 'ng' with your mouth open. I call it messy because it doesn't need to be perfectly in tune, it doesn't need to be even, and most of all I don't want you to be bossy. Remember not to go up and down with the pitch. Your posture is now correct so just maintain that sense of poise. It doesn't need to be loud; it's not about tone or volume, it's just about pitch-flexibility. I would like you to have the sense that it is your imagination that is enabling your hum to take this particular route from the first pitch to the last. Unlike playing an instrument, and don't let anybody tell you that the voice is an instrument, there is virtually no physicality involved apart from that sense of poise that comes from holding the posture that we have learned.

Messy scale
figure 1

This sliding between notes seems so radical, can it possibly be right? Yes, it's right and it is the very essence of singing. And there's a word for it: *legato*. Working with a professional choir in Germany I was once asked specifically to work on their sound. At first I thought how am I going to do that? In fact, it wasn't difficult, because once I was insisting on *legato*, every aspect of their sound benefited. This Italian word literally means 'bound together', and the Italian teachers in the seventeenth century, around the time of the birth of Opera, would say to their students *"Chi non lega, non canta"*. Literally, he who doesn't bind, doesn't sing; or, if it's not *legato*, it isn't singing. I once heard the wonderful French conductor Louis Langrée say this about *legato*: "It isn't two notes, it's one note that changes."

So, a keyboard player can't play *legato* in the sense that there is no way of getting in the spaces between the notes. A string player can. However, don't be misled! Our impression of the string player's *legato* can be that it is achieved by pressure, the pressure of the bow on the string and of the fingers going up and down the fingerboard. This is no help to the singer. We've already seen how the voice, even the hum, should not be pushed. So if *legato* singing isn't to do with pressure what is it to do with? It's to do with openness and here's my most golden of golden principles:

You should aim to sing *legato* all the time and the key to *legato* singing is the open throat.

For instrumentalists *legato* is one of a multitude of Italian terms you can apply or not to the music being played. Not for the singer. You should aim to sing *legato* all the time. We haven't sung at all yet, we've just hummed, and in order to turn humming into singing we open not just the mouth, we have hummed with an open mouth, but the throat.

Opening the throat

Have a yawn. You have opened the throat. Have a snore. The fleshy muscle that seems to be making the sound is the soft-palate. I refer to this for obvious reasons as the snoring muscle. So, the yawny open throat position is achieved by lifting the snoring muscle and keeping the tongue low and therefore out of the way. This yawny position is the basis for the Ah vowel on which we will now sing our descending messy scale, as with the hummed version, starting on A flat and going up a semitone at a time. Remember to stay tall as you sing this descending phrase. You will be tempted to descend with it. I frequently see a room full of people all descending together. We've already identified this hazard with our hummed descending scale but now we also have to keep the throat open all the way down. When you remember to do this the sound is transformed and you produce quality not just at the top but through the middle of the range and at the bottom, and you are not tempted to push or drive the lowest notes. Again, you have a sense that the right approach enables you to let something happen, rather than that you need to make it happen. We instinctively think that the top of the voice is the important bit, and concentrate less hard and try less hard, when we're not singing high notes. But everything matters even in the simplest exercise, or we wouldn't be doing it. We can all name singers with fantastic high notes, but the really great singers are making a wonderful sound even in the 'uninteresting' parts of the range, compelling us to listen to every syllable. So stay tall and keep your throat open for the whole descending messy scale.

I find it helpful to refer to the Ah vowel as the organ pipe vowel, and to tell singers who are trying too hard and doing too much, that they should think of themselves as organ pipes. You are just a pipe with a hole, and organ pipes don't move much. Remember, it's the opening and keeping open of the throat that is crucial, rather than the mouth, which obviously is open but will largely take care of itself when other factors are right. I find an age-old piece of advice helpful here; that you should look like the village idiot, and smile. We will come back to the jaw, but we are looking at the village idiot as the exemplar of the free jaw and the smile as a way of lifting the facial muscles, immediately brightening the tone and engaging the listener.

The Roger Moore

The origin of this exercise is a matter of some uncertainty, in fact I believe it may have started life as a joke. However, I find it extremely useful in demonstrating and experiencing the feeling that only the note moves while we stay still. The idea is that Roger Moore, an actor famous for playing James Bond, orders a drink and somehow this becomes a vocal exercise involving the whole of one's vocal range. You say "Bottle of Raspberry Tizer please" starting on your lowest note, reaching your highest note on the first syllable of "Tizer," then returning to your lowest. We tend to do unhelpful even counterproductive things at the extremities of our vocal range, and this is probably going to be demonstrated by the first attempt at this exercise. We tend to tuck the chin in for low notes, it doesn't achieve anything except close the throat which is the last thing we should be doing. We tend to reach for high notes, possibly lifting the chin. Again, nothing positive happens and we lose that all important openness of the throat. So, only the note moves. The instructions "Don't dig for the bottle, or reach for the Tizer" make a world of difference. And everyone is smiling!

I'm using the word openness a lot, principally about the throat, but there is also an openness about the face and body when we're performing crucial to our relationship with an audience. A singing pupil of mine who also practised martial arts told me that in martial arts, openness is strength. As soon as I heard this I wanted to use exactly the same expression for singing. Openness is strength. That openness might make you feel vulnerable, but embrace it with courage! You will feel the strength and you will be taking a giant leap forward.

The Ah vowel is a very good place to start! So much of the time, particularly in English, we are singing on an Ah vowel or a minor modification of it. This can be surprising as the spelling of words in English obeys no rules. I once arrived late for rehearsals of Michael Tippett's oratorio *A Child of Our Time* in Leipzig, and the choir's accompanist had had to start the rehearsals on his own. He didn't speak very much English. The work opens with the words "The world turns"; only three short words but a pronunciation minefield if you don't speak English. I was able of course to help them very easily and I squirrelled it away as an example of what I've said about the Ah vowel and its minor modifications. Can they really all be Ah vowels? No, but they are all very close and it gets you off to a good start.

Our descending messy scale on the Ah vowel is now going well. But there's one thing we haven't talked about, and it's possibly the most important part of anything we do: how we begin.

Establishing the right sense of direction

It has surprised people that I ask them to sing in the space between the notes. Do you mean actually slide between the notes they sometimes ask. Yes, I do. And here's the other big surprise. You need a sense of direction when you are singing, and that sense of direction is towards you rather than away from you. In other words, if you are singing in an auditorium and your voice is travelling from you on stage to the audience, the sense of direction it is most helpful for you to feel can be indicated by an arrow from the audience to you. With the feel that comes from this sense of direction, comes a sense that you are drawing their attention towards you, keeping them interested and increasingly involved in the story you are telling. Have you ever attended a performance where you felt you were being assaulted? That's the danger when the sense of direction is the wrong way round, and of course the singer is tempted to push the voice, something that we have already seen needs to be avoided. Finally, both in the short term, the duration of that particular performance, and the long term, the decades of singing you should be able to enjoy, the wrong way round is tiring and possibly even vocally damaging. Incidentally, this idea is not only helpful for singers, but also for teachers and lecturers faced with a hall full of students whose attention they need to hold, and to whom they need to get their ideas across without tiring their voices out.

The start of the note or onset

When I saw the wonderful Scottish singing teacher Patricia MacMahon paw the air in front of her to demonstrate the start of the note or onset, it didn't occur to me that that gesture, the stroke as I began to call it, would be utterly central to my teaching and choir training. But there it is, a gesture to go with the idea. Performing this simple gesture and having the sense that you are stroking the vowel into the space, the space being the open throat, transforms the tone quality from something ordinary to something vibrant and engaging. This is proved every time I warm up a choir with whom I'm working for the first time. I get them to sing an Ah vowel in the middle of the range, then I get them to do it having introduced them to the stroke; it immediately sounds and feels totally different. If a sung note starts abruptly and not beautifully you can rectify it straight away by saying "You're switching on a light when you should be stroking a pussycat". The stroke is dead easy but some people might not get it right to begin with. The sense of direction needs to be right of course: towards you. It must not be too gentle, it needs conviction, and finally, the timing must be right: silence becomes sound when the fingers come into contact with the fur. Every single starting note will benefit from this idea: from high and loud, where you are tempted to try too hard and sacrifice quality and intonation, to low and quiet where even at the most petrifying of moments it will provide the right energy to get started. It's always a pussycat. The singers in your choir can use this gesture in rehearsal but they can't do it in the concert of course. They won't need to. They will be able to think it, and that thought combined with the memory of having done it right so many times in rehearsal will be enough. They can't do it in the concert but you can. A Russian student once approached me for advice on choral conducting. He was singing in an international student choir in Germany which I was chorusmastering. He showed me a film of his conducting and his first gesture was unmistakably a stroke. I talked about this to another Russian student and she pointed to the middle of the palm of her hand and said that this part of the hand, according to the great tradition of conductor training in St Petersburg, was of crucial importance to the conductor's expressive powers. A further thought, which I find fascinating and inspiring, is that in Reflexology, the complementary therapy based on the theory where points on the hands (and feet) correspond to parts of the body, this part of the hand corresponds to the solar plexus, our emotional core. Crucially, the techniques of singing and choral conducting overlap in this gesture.

The lifting of the hand before the stroke needs care; it's the upbeat and therefore the breathing in in preparation to sing. Before that first note, when do we breathe, and how much air do we need to take in? The timing and proportion of what we are doing with our hand are a great help in answering these questions. You are unlikely to breathe too early or too late, or to take in too much air, something we are often tempted to do at the start of a long phrase. As we breathe in through the mouth it's crucial that we have a sense of opening the throat and preparing the space, the space being that yawny Ah shape, regardless of what our first vowel might be. After the stroke, once you have started the note, just let your hand drop gently by your side; if it gets stuck in front of you the sound will get stuck too.

Having sung messy scales on the Ah vowel it's time to sing messy *arpeggios*, see figure 2. As previously stated, it's crucial to remember just how different the singing voice is from the keyboard. Don't listen to the keyboard version first with its smug, perfectly in tune four notes. Rejoice in the singer's version! It's not four separate notes, it's one big shape in which the four notes of the *arpeggio* can be identified, but it's *legato* in a way that the keyboard never can be. Always practise *arpeggios* the down and up way round and make sure you stay tall and that the throat stays open. Remember there needs to be a sense of letting it happen rather than making it happen.

We have so far only sung the Ah vowel. To me it's the obvious place to start and it's pretty close to the first sound we ever made! Before we go on to the others let me say something about the jaw. The jaw is a big bone and bone resonates, so surely it must be an important resonator. I'm fairly sure that if you suspended a human jaw bone and struck it with a beater it would not sound like a bell. However, the jaw plays a crucial role in singing and it's important that we deal with it correctly.

I ask my choirs and singing classes a question: "Do you want to be a pinger or a doinker?". Naturally enough they look rather uncomprehending. So I take a large wine glass, hold it upside down by the base and flick it. It pings. Then I hold onto the part of the glass that holds the liquid and flick it again. It doinks. I repeat my question and they all say "Pinger!". The resonating glass is the jaw. We have all seen singers with their jaws held. It doesn't look very good and it certainly doesn't sound good. The trick with the wine glass may not literally reproduce what happens when we sing, but it makes the point that the jaw needs to be free. We can all hear that the tension involved when the jaw is held is clearly inhibiting something, stopping something happening and of course we are very much in the business of letting something happen.

I've used the word tension for the first time and it's important to know that in singing, as everywhere else, there is desirable tension and undesirable tension. There can be so much emphasis on being relaxed when making music that the fact that some tension is necessary gets overlooked. You're standing up; if you were completely relaxed you would be lying down. And of course there's no music, or even sound, without tension; think of a piano, the strings on a violin or the skin of a drum. The posture that we have learned, the lifted soft palate, the fact that we defy gravity by staying tall throughout a slow, quiet, descending phrase; all these involve desirable tension.

The five vowels

Let's look at the five vowel sounds which I will write as Ah, Eh, Ee, O (as in song) and Oo for our exercises.

Standing tall singing an Ah vowel, I want you to think of a North/South feel in terms of how you visualise what you are doing with North as up and South as down. I want you to keep that North/South feel for all the vowels. You can sing them all with minimal modification to the shape of your mouth. From Ah to Eh there's a feeling that the space is the same but the shape is slightly modified. You will feel the tongue getting involved in the Ee vowel but resist the temptation to involve the jaw and make sure you keep the North/South feel. O will feel very close to Ah, and the change from O to Oo can be achieved with very little involvement of the lips; too much involvement of the lips is wasted effort and creates unnecessary tension. I think of the palette of sung vowels as occupying a fraction of the space that the spoken vowels occupy. This is a unifying element in singing but not necessarily something the listener is aware of. A teacher of mine used to say the vowels are not near neighbours, they are all in the same house.

We can now sing our down/up *arpeggio* on all five vowels and you should get a real sense of the vowels feeling similar but still sounding distinct. It's so tempting to overdo the differences between them in an attempt to be expressive, but this can create a very exaggerated effect and should be reserved for moments of caricature. Because openness is so crucial to singing and the Ee vowel can easily not be open enough, I think of it as the most important vowel to get right. If you can maintain openness on your Ee vowel then everything will have that North/South feeling, and your vowels will all be in good shape. Now you can sing all five vowels one after the other in our messy *arpeggio*:

Messy *arpeggio*

figure 2

Ah_____ Eh_____ Ee_____ O_____ Oo_____

It's not an easy exercise. *Arpeggios* are hard to sing, we were not designed to sing them. The clue is in the word; *arpeggiare* meaning to play the harp, a close relative of the keyboard instrument. So, it's not easy but it's a great exercise and it does get easier if you are doing it regularly. In fact the expression "five a day" as far as I'm concerned refers to your five vowel *arpeggios*. There's another reason why it's not easy; it's a long phrase! And you probably feel that you are running out of breath at the end. I'm constantly telling singers that they are not running out of breath, rather, they are losing the good posture they have at the beginning of the phrase, or in this case, exercise, and letting themselves collapse, probably by only a centimetre or two but it's enough to spoil everything. Beware gravity! It's relentless. And stay tall. When you do remember to stay tall, towards the end of the exercise you will feel your belly-dancing muscles getting involved. "Are they saying hello?", I often ask, and if they are, you know you're doing it right and you feel a real sense of connection between body and voice. And if you stay tall you will find you can sing longer phrases.

So far, all that has been said about sense of direction relates to the start of the note or onset. Having got off to the best possible start we now need to know how to continue. The magic words are *inalare la voce* meaning inhale the voice, another pearl from the *bel canto* teaching tradition; the direction of flow continues to be towards you, or more helpfully, into you. To make friends with this idea, create a clockwise circular motion with the index finger of your right hand, alongside your face.

Doing the action quickly, at least two revolutions per second, gives your singing a sense of dynamism which doesn't change, however loud, soft, fast, slow, high or low you are singing. A sense of this makes a world of difference in all manner of contexts. A high, exposed entry on a sustained note, as in the final movement of Brahms's *Ein deutsches Requiem*, is nerve-wracking indeed, particularly at the end of a long performance. But now you have something helpful to think about. You won't feel stuck. You will have practised it many times with your finger whizzing round, and now you can incorporate that idea into your singing without actually doing it. The sound is transformed and now you can even *crescendo* or *diminuendo* on the sustained note. The sense of direction and a sense of dynamism have changed everything.

Happy Seals

figure 3

Ah_____

One of the benefits of naming exercises is that you can identify them easily. Another benefit of giving them names like this, is that it shows you are not taking yourself too seriously; I find in most situations that goes down well. This is an *inalare la voce* exercise. It can be done on all vowels and with either five or eight repeated notes in the middle. You can also join up the repeated notes to make one long note in the middle on which you can *crescendo* and *diminuendo*. Finally, you can make the whole thing a *crescendo* or *diminuendo*. You can achieve a great deal with this exercise; essentially, you are exercising the voice while getting used to the *inalare la voce* feel with all types of phrase. You can even turn it upside down. I have occasionally been asked why it's called Happy Seals but I'm hoping it's fairly obvious.

Long yawny scales

figure 4

Ah_____

Eh_____ etc.

Let's recall the idea of not following the pitch around with our heads and bodies. Instinctively we do it. I find if I'm reading a difficult angular line in a piece of contemporary music it's a trap I can very easily fall into. You will see plenty of singers doing it at the extremes of the range. It doesn't help. Singing long scales, to the ninth and down again twice on all vowels, is not only a good exercise for reminding people not to bob up and down, it's also a great energiser. Start on a B flat so that everyone is comfortable, move up by semitones, and with a four part choir sit the altos and basses down when you've covered all five vowels and one extra Ah (after the scale starting on

E flat). You can carry on with the sopranos and tenors taking them to the top of their ranges. The ascending part of the scale will require a feeling of yawny space, hence the name of the exercise. The crucial thing is that that openness is not lost in the descent.

Now you're ready for anything. With a choir used to this kind of warm-up it should take a maximum of fifteen minutes.

In the following chapters I deal with what happens next. The warm-up has taught the choir sound singing technique or at least reminded them of the essentials. It has also provided terms of reference which you can use. There are things that can only be properly understood in their context, so here are some contexts where some of us spend much of our working lives. And what a privilege that is!

3

Rehearsing *The Evening Primrose*
No.4 of *Five Flower Songs*
Op.47 by Benjamin Britten

Close attention to detail in this short four part piece will reveal a multitude of points which you will encounter again and again in the choral repertoire. We get a long way by identifying these and deciding how to rehearse them.

Rehearsing is about getting the details right but also about building confidence, and your choir will need confidence for this perfect miniature. First of all, a general point: some choral music is very quiet (a high proportion of this piece) and some is extremely loud. I suggest that you start by ignoring the printed dynamics and rehearse *mp/mf*. In quiet music this enables the singers to get comfortable with the notes, words and rhythms without trying to sing impossibly quietly while still learning; in loud music it stops them wearing their voices out. It's also essential to go one step at a time. Start with the rhythm. In *The Evening Primrose* the opening rhythm will recur several times during the course of the piece, so get your choir used to its gentle syncopation by just asking them to speak the rhythm quietly but accurately as far as "west" which you will shorten to a dotted crotchet/quarter-note in order to allow a breath before the next line. Harmonically this piece is not terribly complicated. Often, expressive harmonic effects are achieved by a composer simply adding a note or more than one note to a common chord. First of all therefore, you must encourage your choir to get really comfortable with common chords. So, at the opening, just sing as far as "the" perfectly in tune and in the rhythm that you have already rehearsed. "Perfectly in tune"; that's a challenge, so let's see how to do it. I have already talked about one step at a time, to get a chord perfectly in tune this is how we'll work. Start with one part, or in this case two parts because sopranos and altos both sing the same F sharp. Get them to sustain it until it is so well in tune that they look at each other as if to say "It's never felt like this before!" The rest of the choir will listen in admiration. Next, add the B the tenors sing and wait for the same reaction. Then add the D sharp the basses sing. Then sing the next chord without its added note which is the sopranos' F sharp. Then add the F sharp. Then ask the choir to sing the next chord without the tenors' A natural, then add it. All the time you are building up slowly and making friends with the piece and its particular challenges.

There are questions we need to address about pronunciation and articulation. There can be no definitive guide to the pronunciation of languages when sung, because depending on how fast or slow you are singing, how high or low, how loud or soft, there will be a limit to what's possible, necessary or desirable, certainly in terms of how the consonants are pronounced. The important thing is that the listener has every chance of hearing the words. This won't always require the careful pronunciation of every single consonant; in a fast passage this is simply not possible and just amounts to wasted effort. In the third bar are we going to elide the d at the end of "and" and the d of "dew-drops"? The choir is singing slowly enough to sing both d's and it makes the words clear and expressive. So, let's hear both d's. You can see how this wouldn't be possible or necessary in much faster music. Look at the tied quaver/eighth-note at the end of the ATB "breast". What does this mean? Is the composer asking us to put the final consonant on this note or on the rest which immediately follows? There will always be a healthy difference of opinion over this. Again, context is important; looking at this case I would ask ATB to sing that tied note. I like the overlap it gives you as the sopranos take over the alto F sharp; the same thing will happen at the end of the piece. You can enjoy getting the sopranos and altos really comfortable with the two part section "Almost as pale as moonbeams are, Or its companionable star". Its gentle syncopation has by this point become very natural. Make sure the altos are audible when they come in at "Or its companionable star". They come in on the same note and almost the same vowel that the sopranos are sustaining and their first note can easily be lost. There is no rest for the sopranos in the first bar of the second page (page 18) but it makes sense for them to breathe at the comma, a quaver/eighth-note breath; it will make the short *pp* phrase which follows easier. The minim/half-note before the *Tutti* entry needs to be shortened to a dotted crotchet/quarter-note in order for sopranos and altos to breathe.

There's another decision to make about the words in the next bar; how do we make the words clear at "The evening"? A glottal between the two ee sounds will make the words and the rhythm clear; it mustn't be overdone though, and comparing it to a string player's change of bow can be very helpful. Britten now trusts the tenors with "Its delicate blossoms to the dew". They shouldn't breathe before this phrase. They will appreciate your saying that this moment is all about them! It's their moment but eventually they will still only be singing *p* with accompanying voices singing *ppp*. Notice the tied quaver/eighth-note for SAB at the end of "anew"; you add refinement by singing this note and not coming off on the downbeat. What does the comma mean at the end of the page? It just means take a little time before the new bar, but I would still shorten the tenors' last note of the page as we have at similar moments before.

On the third page (page 19) life seems to get a little more complicated largely because of the presence of accidentals, in particular, double sharps. In fact, it's quite straightforward. The descending interval for the sopranos is a perfect 4th followed by a semitone step up. The ascending interval for the basses is a perfect 5th followed by a semitone down. I would encourage the altos and basses to use a square bracket to remind them of the semitones in their parts, and the tenors will need to concentrate on keeping their G sharp in tune. As repeated notes tend to go flat (I blame gravity!) it's a good idea to think of each repetition a little higher. I often say "add a few extra Herz" to each one to keep it in tune. You can do something with the *tenuto* on "shunning"; but it's a lengthening rather than an accent. A quaver/eighth-note breath after "light" is an option but make sure the *crescendo* on the next chord starts at *pp*. Having used the square bracket as a semitone reminder, an arrow up (or down) over the note can remind you of a tone, in this case over the soprano part on "fair" to show that E sharp to F double sharp is a tone. In the bottom line tune "night" in the way that we have done before: bass D, tenor D, soprano A and finally the third, the alto F sharp. It will now be easy to tune the previous chord "the" with its added C sharp in the tenor part. It may also be helpful here to put an arrow up over the alto F sharp and a square bracket linking the tenor C sharp to the D. To elide or not to elide at "blindfold to"? Singing the final d of "blindfold" and the t can work but it mustn't be overdone. On the other hand, if you elide I think the words are still clear. So it can be a case of listening to both and then making a decision. There's nothing wrong with doing that in a rehearsal as long as you don't do it all the time and as long as you are absolutely clear when you've made your decision. You can't have decided everything before the first rehearsal and it never hurts to show some humility! Make sure these *pp* soprano, alto and bass lines are *legato*; it's so easy to sound as if you are picking the notes out on a xylophone with a melodic shape like this. The notes look short but the key is to find the length in them without slowing down; to sing them *legato sostenuto* even though it's very quiet and delicate. And remember, when you find the length, you find the quality! Make sure the basses don't go digging for the low notes here; they should be just as tall at the bottom of the phrase as they were at the top. And the final bass note will need to be shortened in the usual way.

In a piece which has barely got above *p* at last at "Thus it blooms..." we have a *crescendo*. It is not marked but I suggest starting this line *pp* and even though in the original this doesn't quite appear to be a two bar *crescendo*, it probably should be; the important thing is not to get too loud too soon. There are lots of Ah vowels contained in the words "while night is by" and Ah is the ideal *crescendo* vowel. There is no rest before the *f* "When day looks out..." but a quaver/eighth-note breath works well. Don't overdo the accent on "day". Three out of four parts rise to this chord so it will be louder anyway. It's an accent but it's within *f* not *ff* and of course, it's always a pussycat. The same goes for "open". Let's do exactly what the composer asks for in the remainder of this phrase. You will hear recordings of choirs breaking before "'Bashed", short for abashed (embarrassed, confused, ashamed), and you will hear that note accented. However, clearly Britten just wants a long *diminuendo* and an unbroken phrase. It's a long phrase so the breathing will have to be worked out, but it will be very effective.

The piece has, as you would expect, an exquisitely delicate conclusion. Remember to rehearse the final section "It faints and withers..." at *mp/mf* long before you try to achieve the printed *pp* and *ppp*. Rehearse the soprano/tenor and bass/alto canons in unison to get them perfectly in tune and matching before singing them as written, and stop on unisons that are not perfectly in tune even if you are only asking for two notes; so sustain "faints" until it's in tune, then sustain "and" until it's in tune and so on. Working on the soprano "and" in the last line with *inalare la voce* will give it a much needed sense of direction and help it to be *legato*. Start rehearsing this final soprano phrase *mf* until they are happy with it, then get it gradually quieter and quieter. The composer puts *ppp* in brackets; he knows he's asking a lot! I would recommend a little slowing down in the bar before the end and a quaver/eighth-note breath for the tenors; it looks like another tenor moment but it actually isn't; they mustn't stand out this time. And finally, make sure there is somewhere to go in the last bar so that we hear a *diminuendo*.

Wow! You are asking a lot from your choir. But if you don't ask you certainly won't get; and now you know exactly what to ask for.

THE EVENING PRIMROSE
Op.47, No. 4

words by John Clare   music by Benjamin Britten

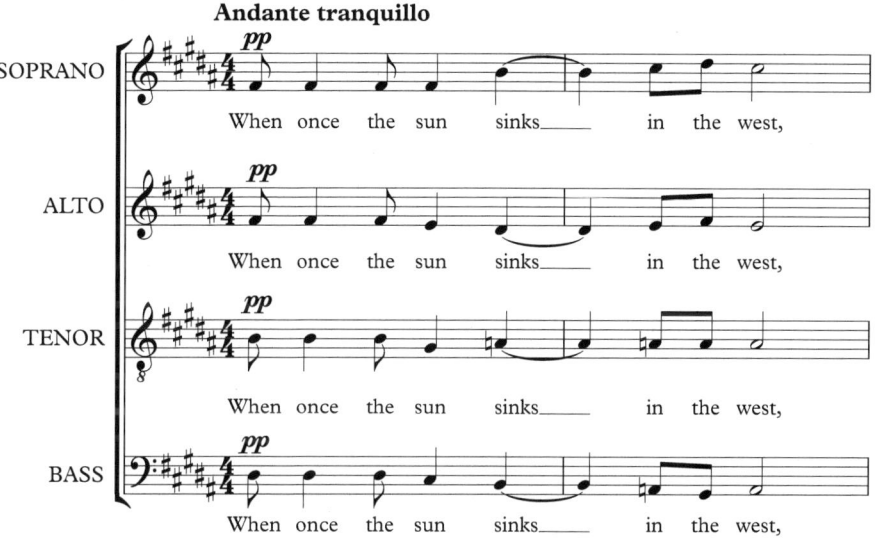

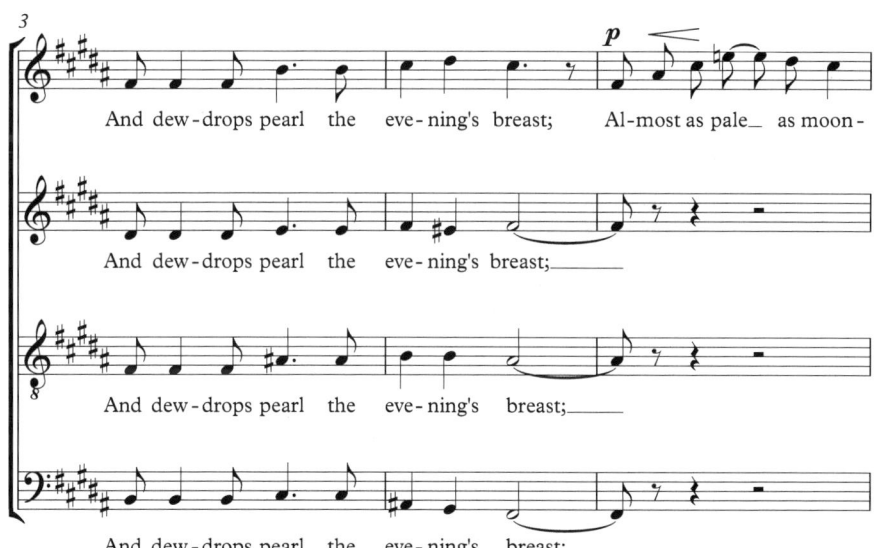

Copyright ©1951 by Boosey & Co. Ltd
Reprinted with permission under licence from Boosey & Hawkes Ltd

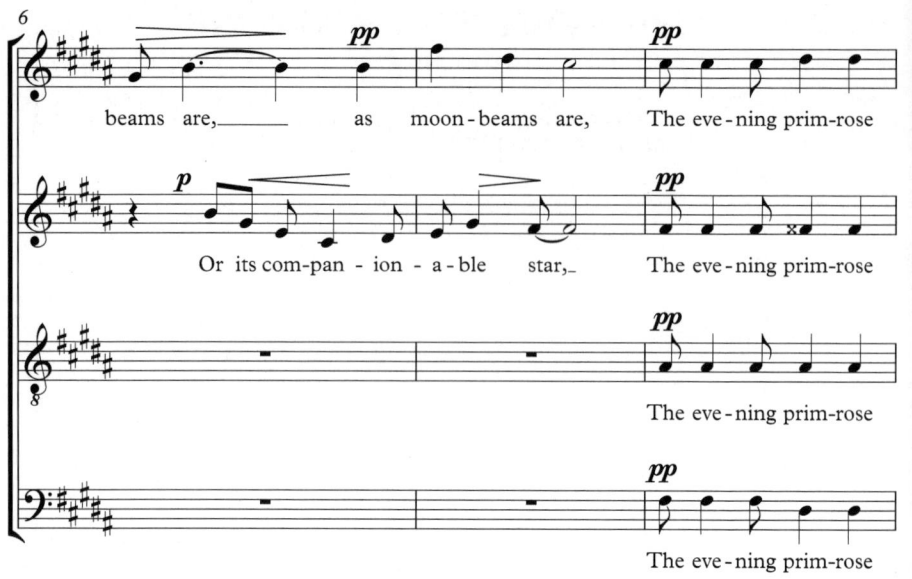

12
pp
cresc.
And, her - mit- like, shun - ning the light, Wastes its fair bloom up -
And, her - mit- like, shun - ning the light, Wastes its fair bloom up -
And, her - mit- like, shun - ning the light, Wastes its fair bloom up -
And, her - mit- like, shun - ning the light, Wastes its fair bloom up -

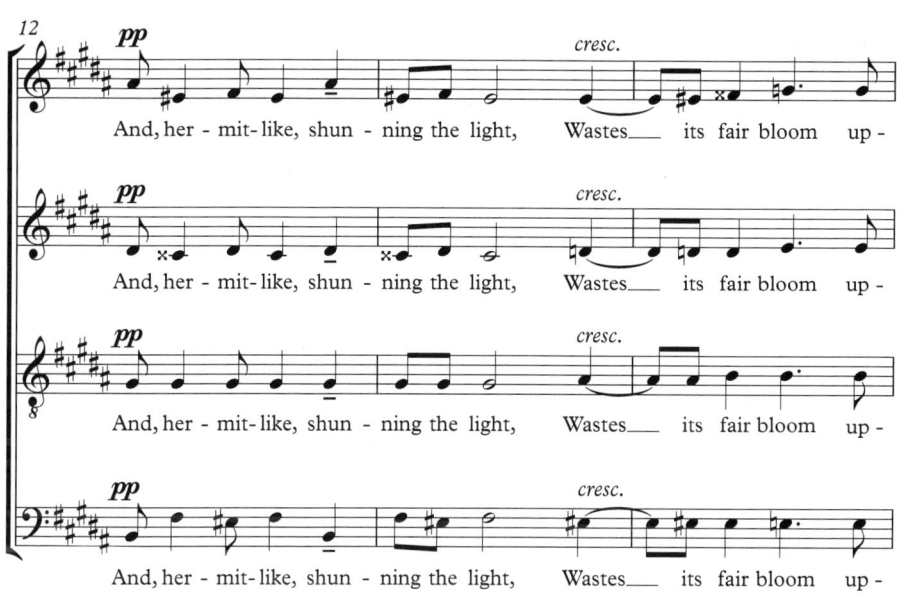

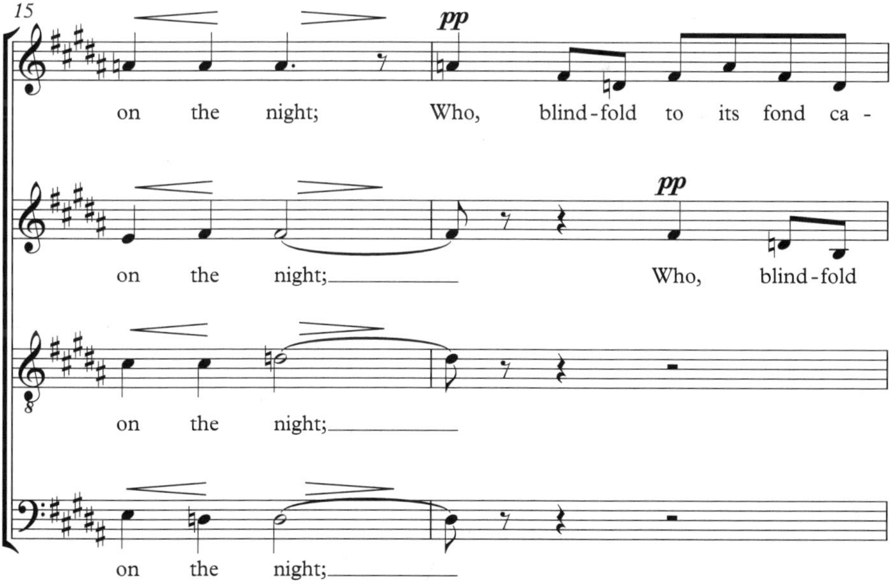
15
pp
on the night; Who, blind-fold to its fond ca -
on the night; Who, blind-fold
on the night;
on the night;

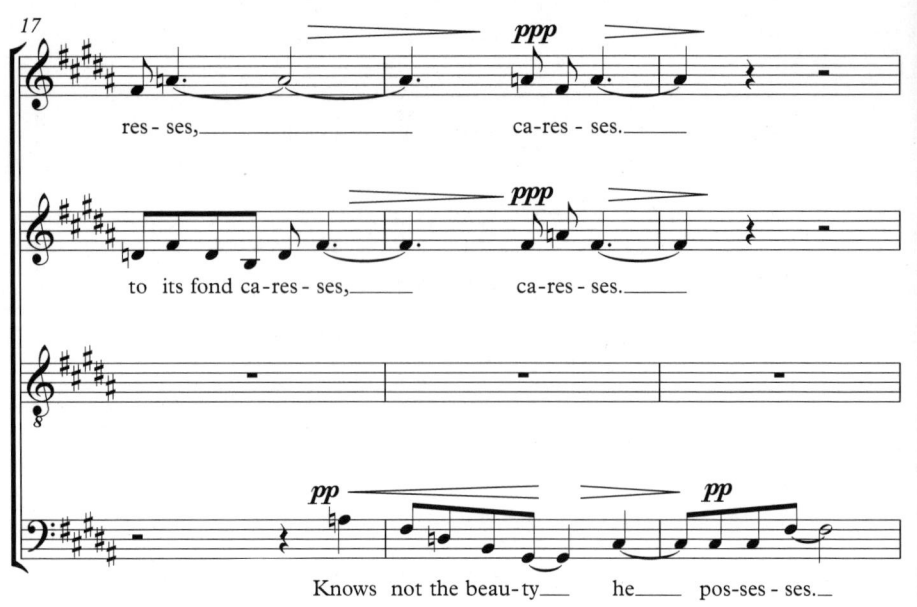

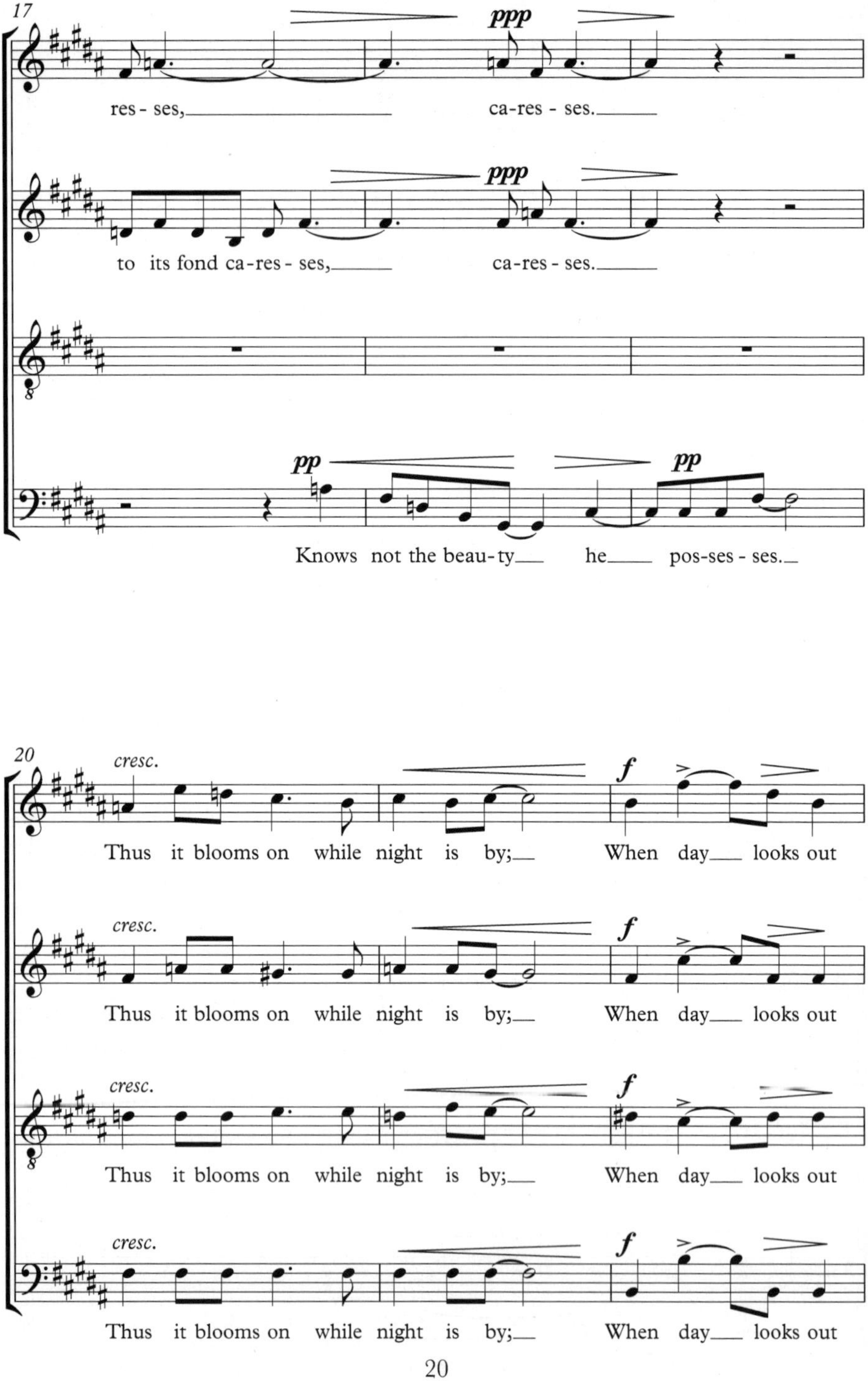
17
ppp
res - ses, ca-res - ses.
ppp
to its fond ca-res - ses, ca-res - ses.
pp pp
Knows not the beau-ty he pos-ses - ses.
20
cresc.
f
Thus it blooms on while night is by; When day looks out
cresc.
f
Thus it blooms on while night is by; When day looks out
cresc.
f
Thus it blooms on while night is by; When day looks out
cresc.
f
Thus it blooms on while night is by; When day looks out

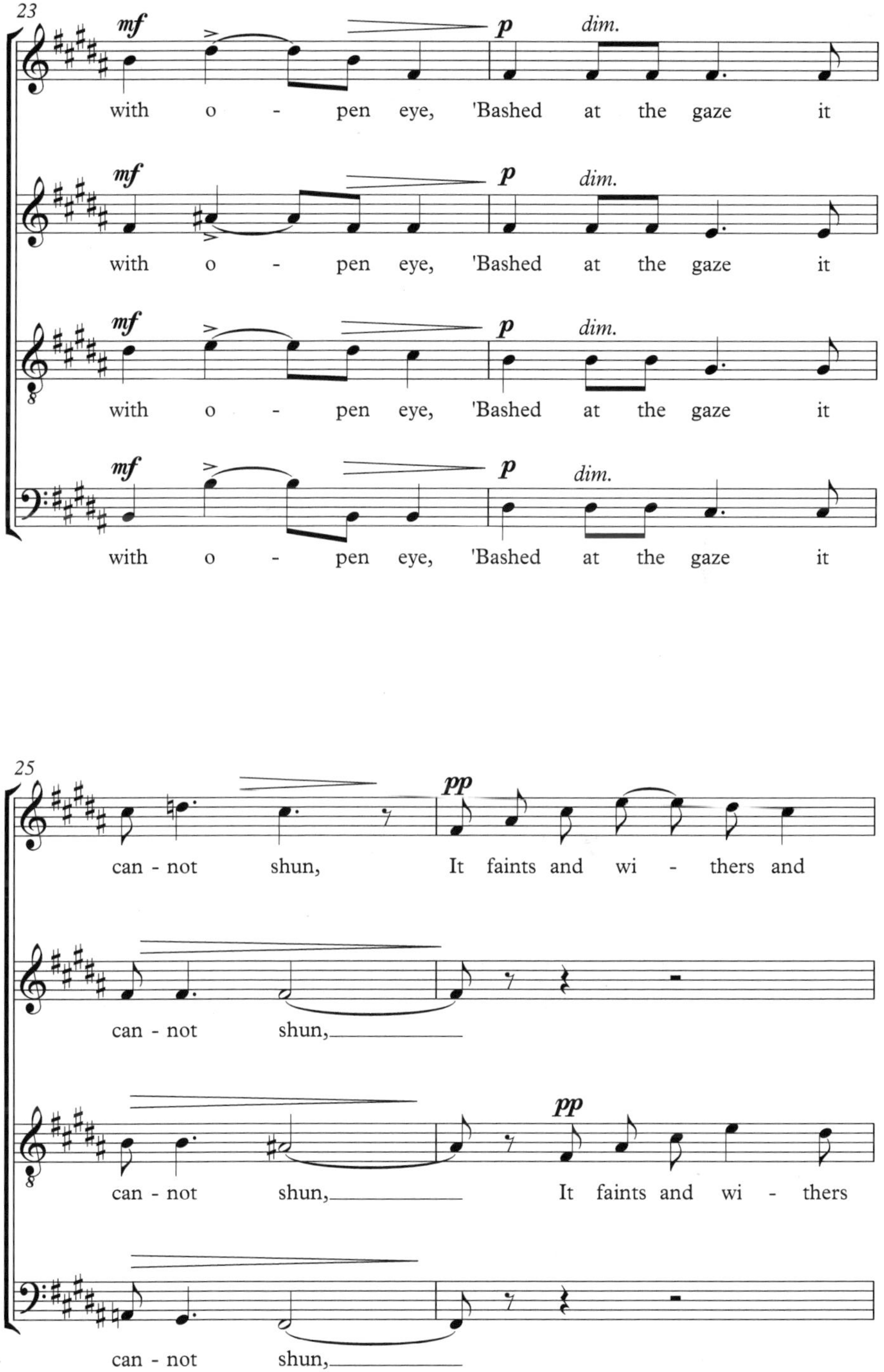

27
is gone It faints and wi - thers and
pp
It faints and wi - thers and is gone
and is gone It faints and wi - thers
pp
It faints and wi - thers and is gone,
29
(ppp)
is gone, and is gone.
It faints and wi - thers and is gone.
and is gone It faints and is gone.
It faints and wi - thers and is gone.

4

Tips for preparing Handel's *Messiah*

No. 4. And the glory of the Lord
The articulation of the instrumental introduction does not need to be imitated by the chorus; you can pick up their energy but still sing *legato*. Not singing *legato* will have the effect of compromising vocal quality. Initially, this commitment to *legato* nearly always slows things down, but that's easy to fix. There can be a wonderfully poetic contrast between the *Tutti* "And the glory of the Lord" and the overlapping lines "shall be revealed". At "and all flesh shall see it together" there are two elision possibilities; I suggest that you don't need two lots of sh and that the Italianate double t, I sometimes refer to it as the spaghetti t, will work at "it together". Tenors and basses may be tempted to sing too loudly at "for the mouth...". It's always a pussycat. This will stop that judder you so often get on the first note at moments like this where it takes time for the pitch to settle; it will also improve the tone on this sustained A by establishing the right sense of direction for the *inalare* feel. There's always a danger in triple time that the first beat of the bar becomes accented giving it the feeling of a rather unsophisticated dance! So, I always look for interesting things to do on beats 2 and 3: for example "and <u>all</u> flesh shall see it <u>to</u>gether". John Butt, Professor of Music at Glasgow University and great Bach expert can often be heard saying "Go easy on the downbeat, it has gravity on its side!". The soprano top A is a wonderful moment and it should be tremendously satisfying to work on. Always make friends with high notes and high passages by singing them to Ah first. There can then be a sense that you've got comfortable up there before singing the words. It might feel like a trick but I will sometimes get a soprano section to sing a note such as that top A without reminding them about *inalare la voce*. Then I get them to sing it with the whizzing finger; night and day!

Charles Villiers Stanford used to give this movement to his composition students as an object lesson in what can be achieved with four voices and accompaniment. We know it so well that it's hard to see it with fresh eyes but I do think Stanford had a point; it's perfect!

No. 7. And he shall purify
Everybody's first note, particularly the sopranos', is hard to sing in tune; short notes always are. And *Messiah* is full of upbeats which string players, and keyboard players, only need to touch for them to be exquisitely in tune. But singers need to find all the length they can even in a note as short as this; and then they need to do it without getting behind! Think your way through the semiquavers/sixteenth-notes. Refer back to the feel of random humming. That flexibility is the basis of *coloratura* singing. It needs no

physicality apart from the open throat and staying tall. And here's some good news: the last syllable of "purify" is an Ah.

No. 12. For unto us a child is born
Make sure this opening theme doesn't feel like a xylophone solo! Even the short notes are long! I sometimes throw a singer an imaginary ball of pizza-dough and say "Knead that!". I want the singer to pull it apart on every note to create a feeling of length on short notes. It works like a charm. And when you find the length, you find the quality. Often, initially a singer will work too hard at the words in the pizza-dough version but you can point this out and it should no longer be a problem. It reminds me of a question that rattled around my brain for some time: why shouldn't choral conductors mouth the words? I had a feeling it was wrong but it took me a while to decide why. If the conductor mouths the words he/she will tend to do it in an exaggerated way and the choir will start exaggerating too, which will have a detrimental effect on their singing. It's very tempting to mouth the words to children when you are anxious that they might not remember them. But don't do it! Make sure they are completely confident and don't need the help; they will do a better job!

I recommend no r on "for" and a glottal on "unto" for clarity. And here's another opportunity to avoid the obvious and make something interesting happen: "For unto us a <u>child</u> is born". Don't start playing the xylophone at "The mighty God, The everlasting Father", here's that pizza-dough again; find the length in those short notes. I've always enjoyed the fact that this chorus is based on a love duet!

No. 24 Surely he hath borne our griefs
I once heard Andrew Davis say these words to a choir which he attributed to Arturo Toscanini: "Non mangiate le piccole note!" Don't eat the small notes! It's 24 carat gold advice to singers. Also, before the first complete *Ring Cycle* in Bayreuth in 1876, Wagner posted handwritten notices in prominent places backstage for the singers to see. The notice read "Take care of the small notes, the big ones will take care of themselves".

Let's see what they might have said about this chorus. "Surely" has three syllables; I'm really interested in the middle one! Find some length in "he hath"; these notes look so short but you bring the next two bars to life by finding their length and their energy. Time after time we will find that the energy is in the small notes. A few bars later it's the first syllable of "transgressions" that needs length and immediately the word becomes expressive. I've heard "the chastisement" accented in many performances but for me it works so much better sung *legato sostenuto*, providing complete contrast with the scourging motif in the accompaniment.

No. 25 And with his stripes we are healed
As above, I have heard accented versions of this opening motif on many occasions. Here's my alternative: let the *sostenuto legato* be the healing! And dare to do this movement with two beats in the bar rather than four.

No. 28 He trusted in God
Even this can be *legato sostenuto*! It doesn't need to be punchy and *staccato* to be menacing. That version has been around for as long as I can remember with its halved note values at "-light in him". If you want to shorten something, then the previous three notes can be shortened, "if he de-", without contradicting what Handel wrote.

No. 39 Their sound is gone out
Many great singers started out at English National Opera and their names have become well known. A less well-known name however is that of Helen Robertson-Barker who was on the music staff at ENO for many years. I'm sure it's fair to say that those well-known singers and countless others owe a very great deal to the hours spent learning roles with HR-B as she was fondly known. I mention her for one particular reason. If she thought you were working too hard at the words she would say "Text is a four letter word!". She certainly got her point across. Conductors and chorus masters can sometimes be heard asking for more text. It's not always helpful. Of course there will be times when the words aren't clear and an adjustment has to be made but the instruction needs to be specific; for example an elision of consonants might be the problem or the vowel colour might need attention.

The phrase "and their words unto the end of the world" is exactly the kind of moment where we might be tempted to over-pronounce as there are a lot of words to sing quickly. But it will sound choppy and ungainly and will have been wasted effort. Everyone can stay relaxed on these entries; there must be no sense of overworking the syllables. At moments like this, and more challenging moments with even faster words, it's a good idea to keep a small mouth.

No. 41 Let us break their bonds asunder
Handel, one of the greatest ever composers for the voice has asked the orchestra and choir for *Allegro e staccato*. What can he have been thinking about? *Staccato* literally means detached and that's virtually impossible with these leads at this speed. In fact it is impossible. So we need to make sense of what the composer has asked for without attempting the impossible. Often, when a composer asks singers for *staccato* the effect must be achieved by moderately accenting every note. This will work here and ensure that the voices and strings complement each other.

No. 44 Hallelujah
It's so tempting to hit this first syllable really hard; but you now know better of course. And what would Toscanini have said about the semiquavers/sixteenth-notes in the third and forth "Hallelujahs"? It's tempting to go up and down with the pitch at "and he shall reign for ever and ever" but we stay still, only the notes go up and down. "KING OF KINGS"; it's tempting to over-sing again, particularly with those capital letters! But it's always a pussycat and *inalare la voce* is our constant companion.

No. 46 Since by man came death

Why do things go flat? I was once asked this by the chairman of a choir I was conducting. I felt I'd really been put on the spot and without thinking I said "Gravity". Only later did I start to feel satisfied with my answer. If we are really strict with ourselves about posture at a moment like this we are much more likely to stay in tune. If we let ourselves drop then the pitch will drop too. It's also really important not to let the *Grave* sections slow down. At this point in a performance we may just be starting to tire! It would be a good moment to remember that the head is a helium-filled balloon encouraging us to stand to our full height. Don't be tempted to reach for your xylophone beaters at "shall all be made alive". I'd much rather you reached for your pizza-dough. They're short notes but you need to find the length and the quality in them.

No. 53 Worthy is the Lamb

That's no way to treat a pussycat! This opening chord is in my top three moments where it's essential to feel that sense of stroke to get the quality and intonation right. It's particularly tempting for the tenors and basses to hit this first note hard because it's high in the voice and there's nothing quite like reaching the last chorus of a great choral work. But let's not spoil it by over-singing. Bags of conviction of course, but the sense of direction must be right. At this point in the work, when of course we're tired, it's so easy to forget about finding length in the short notes, but there are moments where we really mustn't. At "to receive power..." you can have rehearsed it with the choir just singing the word "long" on each syllable; that will stay in the memory. The same method can be used to rehearse the tenors and basses in the *Larghetto:* "Blessing, and long, long, long, long, long, long, long, long, long, be unto him". That will do the trick. For the rest, the same points just keep needing to be made. The sense of direction on "Amen" can of course go wrong particularly at the *fortissimo Tutti* moments, but you know what to say. When working with the wonderful Canadian conductor Bernard Labadie, a Baroque/Classical specialist, I told him that I spent my life saying six things; he replied that he spent his life saying just three!

5

Tips for preparing Fauré's *Requiem*

I Introit - Kyrie
With the understanding we have gained through our warm-up exercises we now have the means to overcome the challenges in these opening bars. How do we begin? It's always a pussycat. How do we continue? This is possibly the slowest and quietest we will ever be required to sing. *Inalare la voce* is the answer; it gives us a sense of direction and dynamism when the music is almost entirely static. The *crescendo* and *diminuendo* sustained versions of Happy Seals have prepared us for the *crescendo* and *diminuendo* in this opening *Molto largo*. Add refinement by singing the tied quavers/eighth-notes on "luceat" both times.

I need to mention doilies for the first time. The image of the doily, with its holes letting the light through, is helpful for explaining how the punctuation is crucial to clarity both in a single line and in polyphony. From the fifteenth to the sixteenth bar of the *andante moderato* I recommend a very short break for the tenors. The composer hasn't given them a rest but you are probably performing in a resonant building so it won't sound like a rest. It will give the repeated "dona" emphasis and help satisfy the composer's wish for a *crescendo* to *forte*. Even with a single line you can see how the hole in the doily creates just the right amount of transparency. I discourage singing through commas most of the time, but there are exceptions and here's one straight away. It makes sense for the sopranos to sing their first four bars as one phrase without breaking at the comma after "hymnus". It's a short phrase, and unlike the tenor moment above, it doesn't involve a repeated word. To elide or not to elide? There are two answers to this question in the next few bars. In Latin an Italian tt works well at moments such as "et tibi". It works here where one t isn't quite clear enough but two would sound fussy. At "ad te" in the *Tutti* section immediately following, I would recommend the sounding of both consonants; it gives emphasis to "te", an important word in "unto thee shall all flesh come." The extra Herz tip can be given to the tenors now so that their repeated C sharp/D flat stays in tune.

II Offertorium
The further we get of course, it just becomes a matter of applying the same ideas and making case by case decisions. For example, I would elide at "et de profundo"; it's *pianissimo dolcissimo* and smoothness and sweetness go together well here. I love the way Fauré responds to "save them from the lion's mouth", slow, quiet and sweet, the opposite of what other composers have done.

III Sanctus
Elide "Sanctus, Sanctus". I'm contradicting what I said about repeated words in the opening movement, but it's *pianissimo* and it's smooth, and there's no sense of repetition for emphasis; "Sanctus" is always repeated. Again we can add refinement by singing all the tied quavers/eighth-notes in this movement. *Inalare la voce* will transform the "Hosanna" section, and make sure you find some length in the first syllable; when you do, the accented downbeat will take care of itself. I have heard many different versions of the pronunciation of "excelsis", often involving more consonants than absolutely necessary. I favour the "egg shell" version. It's so much more singable, and at the top of the range, certainly for basses here, and *fortissimo*, why make life any harder than it needs to be? Nobody listening is going to be in any doubt about the words here.

V Agnus Dei
Tenors! You've got the hang of it now I'm sure, but just in case anyone needs a reminder, stroking that first note will get you off to the perfect start. Remember, the stroke needs conviction, too gentle and there won't be enough energy, even at *piano dolce*. And once you've begun it's *inalare la voce* all the way. Once the *Tutti* have come in, it's tremendously important in this movement to do exactly what the composer has asked for with the dynamics. If he has written *forte sempre* it's probably because he wants to stop you instinctively making a *diminuendo* before he wants it, and where that *diminuendo* is eventually marked, it's a good idea to write *forte* to remind you that that is the dynamic from which you make the *diminuendo*. It will also stop you making it *subito piano* which is certainly not required.

VI Libera me
A point about the Requiem text that needs to be thought about, is for whom we are actually singing. We start by asking for eternal rest and perpetual light for them. This continues in the Pie Jesu and Agnus Dei. Then, in this setting, it is as if only the baritone soloist has courage enough to contemplate his own death, "Libera me," and having heard him, the choir can admit their own sense of terror at the thought of the day of judgement. The music at "Tremens, tremens factus sum ego" (don't breathe between the two statements of "Tremens", and elide the s's at "factus sum"), tempts us to slow down and get louder in order to be expressive. This is top of my list of things to get right in the Fauré *Requiem*; do exactly as you are asked by the composer! You are too terrified to be expressive! These bars only work at that petrified *pianissimo* and this is the last place you want any sense of *rubato*!

VII In Paradisum
Because it's all about space and openness, sopranos can get off to the best possible start by breathing in on an Ah. This will help not only the first note but also the penultimate syllable of "paradisum" with its rising fourth. This time it's *inalare la voce* all the way for your sopranos which will work particularly well through the *crescendo* to the *forte* F natural at "aeternam". And to keep the sound vibrant in the accompanying voices, it's low, quiet and slow, stay tall, stay open and of course, *inalare* too!

6

Tips for preparing Mozart's *Requiem*

No. 1 Requiem aeternam
This opening *Adagio* provides a wonderful opportunity for *legato sostenuto* singing. There are a number of moments in this work where we can look for an alternative to obvious word stresses and therefore find more interesting musical shapes. Let's start with "et lux perpetua". Rather than stress the third beat of the bar, let's try "et lux per̲petua" and a light really will shine through these two bars. Just as these bars benefit from the pizza-dough treatment for *sostenuto*, so "Exuadi" does, creating maximum contrast with the Baroque dotted rhythm in the orchestra.

In the *Allegro* it's the "ri" in "Kyrie eleison" that energises the word. I'm amazed at how often this opportunity is missed with the little note barely audible. Here this crucial syllable repeats the pitch of the first note so it's no real challenge, but when it's lower as in Haydn's *Missa in Angustiis (Nelson Mass)* it's particularly liable to go missing. Capitalise on these tiny notes every time; it makes a world of difference! Once you have got going with the "C̲h̲r̲i̲s̲-te eleison" leads, as with the semiquaver/sixteenth-note passages in *Messiah* previously discussed, it's the imagination that takes care of the "le-" in "eleison". You cannot imitate the instruments here; the good news is that they double and therefore support you on every one of these leads.

No. 2 Dies irae
Don't be tempted to sing too loudly and sacrifice quality at the start. It's always a pussycat and an open-throated *sostenuto* will be what carries the choral sound over the orchestra here. Find the length in the semiquavers/eighth-notes at "solvet saeclum in favilla, Teste...". In the latter part of the movement I recommend that final notes be shortened for overall clarity in the bass/SAT exchanges at "Quantus tremor est futurus, Dies irae, dies illa," with a hole in the doily for the same reason at the comma in the SAT phrases. I've spotted some tiny notes at the end of the movement; don't let those quavers/eighth-notes in "stric̲t̲e̲" get away!

No. 4 Rex tremendae
Whether this movement is double-dotted or not it's all about the little notes, and even in the hyper-Baroque double-dotted version there's plenty of length to be found. The sopranos in particular have a challenging time in the last three bars. Think pussycat, *inalare la voce* and pizza-dough; pussycat for the first note, stroking the vowel into the open throat, *inalare la voce* for the continuation of the first note, and pizza-dough for that feeling of long, long, long on the quavers/eighth-notes.

No. 6 Confutatis maledictis
Of course I know I'm repeating myself, but listening to recordings while preparing these chapters on core repertoire, I am surprised at what I hear or more accurately don't hear. So the campaign for the reinstatement of short notes goes on. In the opening bass and tenor duelling it's the little notes that count, and you can really make the most of the one in "acribus" with a rolled 'r'! That feeling of length on the quavers/eighth-notes will again make a big difference to how expressive the sopranos and altos can be at "voca me cum benedictis." Extra Herz on repeated pitches will help the basses (and everyone else) stay in tune in the section from "Oro supplex et acclinis," to the end.

No. 7 Lacrimosa
In your first two phrases sopranos, it will help you to sing the A in a way that contains the F. The clue to a high note or a difficult note, this F isn't particularly high or difficult but it's still a good example, can usually be found in the note before. And here you need to sing the A in a way that can match the F you need; you need to sing it lightly. The short notes at "Qua re - sur - get ex fa - vil - la," aren't actually that short at this speed so they will need plenty of length. My only other observation about this movement is that basses sometimes get carried away on their top D seven bars before the end; you know what I'm going to say…

No. 8 Domine Jesu Christe
Let's shorten the last note of "Rex gloriae, Rex gloriae!" in order to get out of the way of the *piano* that follows. And let the comma between the two statements be a hole in the doily; even what seems like a tiny point of articulation makes a difference. Sopranos need to find length and openness in the first note of their "de poenis" both times in order to make the octave leap easier. At "Ne absorbeat eas Tartarus ne cadant in obscurum," the notes go up and down. They go up and down a lot! But we don't. After the short solo quartet section it's so important not to accent the first syllable of "Abrahae". If you start doing it you are stuck with that shape for a long time and it comes back in the next movement. Eventually "Abrahae" will get prominence at the climax of the section, but until then "Quam olim Abrahae promisisti," is more interesting and more elegant.

No. 9 Hostias
I once heard that a choral conductor had screamed "Don't put your name and address on every downbeat!". I'm sure he was driven to it. I'm reminded of it approaching this movement where it's so important to find alternatives to a rather uninteresting one-in-a-bar feel. I'm also keen to avoid any sense of accent on the beautiful dissonance at "laudis". A *hemiola* feel can often come to the rescue in music like this, and that is essentially what's happening if we do this: "Hostias et preces tibi, Domine, tibi, Domine, laudis offerimus;".

No. 10 Sanctus
It's a great pity, to say the least, that we don't have a Sanctus by Mozart! But of course

we are going to sing it beautifully anyway. Tenors and basses you are high in the voice at the start; eschew the temptation to oversing these first notes. It can be even more tempting to make up for the movement's shortcomings at "Pleni sunt coeli.." where some editions have *fortissimo*. There is a moment of glory with the tenors suspended top G in the last bar of the *Adagio*, where for a brief moment we are reminded of Handel at his most opulent. In the Hosanna once more we need to be creative with the phrasing; I suggest "Hosanna in eggshellsis!".

No. 12 Agnus Dei
Only two observations here. The tenor E is a hard note to tune in the third bar and let's have holes in the doily for elegance at the commas between repetitions of "dona".

7

Tips for preparing Beethoven Symphony No.9 *Finale*

The more demanding a work is, the more important it becomes to get the optimum out of your singers, and that effort and energy are not wasted either in rehearsal or performance. In demanding vocal repertoire, both solo and choral, doing it wrong and losing touch with the basic principles quickly tires the voice. So, the challenge in these sixteen minutes' music is to establish and maintain an approach that will make it feel comfortable; highly challenging of course, but doable. It is only this kind of approach that can find the spirit of *An die Freude* or *Ode to Joy*: we certainly don't want the choir to sound anxious or desperate, even if there is an overall sense, as so often in the music of Beethoven, of a struggle overcome. There are many editions of the vocal score and marks of expression differ widely. Always check the vocal score you are using against a full score. You will frequently find inaccuracies which you need to correct before starting work. Full scores vary too, so you need to decide on one as your authority. Bar numbers below refer to Edition Eulenberg 3611.

In loud music it's important that we never lose sight of the difference between *forte* and *fortissimo*, and at *Allegro assai* it's only *forte* however excited the basses are to finally get started, and however commanding the baritone soloist has been. Sometimes the tenors join the basses for these two statements of "Freude!". In the Royal Albert Hall there may be a case for this, it's a vast space to fill, but in general let's stick to what the composer has written. Why not use the tenors here, they're not doing anything else? Simply because if Beethoven had wanted all the male voices singing here he would have scored it accordingly. And it's *f* not *ff*.

There's nothing to suggest that *legato* singing is required when altos, tenors and basses echo the soloist in the next choral entry. Apart from the last note of this eight bar unison passage they are all short notes. It's a trap! Of course it's *legato*! All being well you will be picking up the beautiful *legato* of the soloist, and Schiller's text "Deine Zauber binden wieder", "Your magic reunites us" begs for *legato* singing. And as for short notes...There aren't any short notes! Find the length and you'll find the quality; it's another pizza-dough moment. I suggest breathing after "geteilt;" but you need to be quick in order not to lose the effect of the syncopation.

After sixteen bars from the solo quartet the first choral *Tutti* is anticipated by the basses (bar 48). It's another moment where pitch and quality can suffer if the basses try to sing too loudly and forget the pussycat approach. Everyone needs only to be singing *forte* here, and consciousness of the comma after "Ja", even though there's no time for a breath, will add shape. We have the first of many accents on "nie". Lengthening this note marked *sf* will help the sense of an accent without sacrificing vocal quality, so treat it not just as an accent but as a *tenuto* as well.

In the next choral section (bar 77) we're faced for the first time with the challenge of there not really being anywhere to breathe. Let's therefore put in official breaths after crotchets/quarter-notes with punctuation: after "reben" for altos and basses and after "Tod" for sopranos and basses. Otherwise, let's say breathe where necessary. Let's make "Gott" (bar 84), the first of the minims/half-notes, a dotted crotchet/quarter-note, before deciding how to interpret Beethoven's minims/half-notes with *staccato* dots in the remaining ten bars before the tempo change. Orchestral markings are certainly not always an indication of what the singers should be doing, but here the *ben marcato* for all the instruments with the same note values as the choir is helpful. My suggestion for the choir here is to halve the note values to achieve the *staccato*, and then think *ben marcato*. Having started like this it becomes very effective when STB sing a long "Gott" in the fourth bar (bar 88) followed by a long "steht" for the altos immediately afterwards. There's also a very pleasing contrast between the last two statements of "vor Gott" (bars 91-94). The penultimate statement has a long "vor" and the last statement a short "vor" and usually an extremely long "Gott!".

In the Turkish March, *Allegro assai vivace*, by writing rests, Beethoven has made his own holes in the doily, both for the tenor soloist and in the twenty-one bars for divided tenors and basses which follow. The soloist doesn't always set a good example here but it's essential that the chorus let the daylight in. You need not be too fussy about the note lengths in the bars where Beethoven has written rests; it's a case of singing the shortest note that you can sing in tune. The crucial thing is the hole! The only other observation about this section is to be careful with the *sf* markings on "freudig", "Held" and "Siegen". However joyful, however heroic, however victorious, there always needs to be that sense of stroking the vowel into the open throat.

Most conductors take this section much faster than the printed metronome mark of 84. The beginnings of justification for this might be found in an anecdote about a correspondence between Beethoven and his publisher. The composer submitted a work; the publisher asked for some metronome marks; Beethoven obliged by letter; the letter got lost; Beethoven wrote again; eventually both letters arrived. They weren't the same. I'm reminded of another composer/publisher anecdote. Joy Finzi, the composer Gerald Finzi's widow, and incidentally a wonderful artist, was once asked by a young singer about the printed dynamics in his Shakespeare cycle *Let us garlands bring*. She told him not to take too much notice of them; Finzi hadn't actually written dynamics for the singer, and only added them rather unenthusiastically at the publisher's request. Looking at works such as *The Dream of Gerontius* and *The Kingdom* you can see why Elgar's publisher asked him whether all the marks of expression were really necessary. Elgar is reported to have said rather anxiously "I just want it to be right!".

Back to Beethoven 9 and a great *Tutti* choral entry with the main theme (bar 213). It's only *forte* which makes the *sf* markings easier. Actually, some of these *sf* markings feel very vocal particularly at "feuertrunken" and "Brüder". Breathing in this section can go with the rests with an extra breath both times after "geteilt", making the *fortissimo* on "alle" much easier.

In the *Andante maestoso* it's once again necessary to refer to the full score to see exactly which minims/half-notes have *staccato* dots. Let's also make sure there's no confusion over the meaning of this dot. It means detached but the detachment is only from the note which follows. So, in this case "Seid um" is *legato*, that is *legato* with the glottal before the vowel, distinctive to the German language, which characterises so much of the poem we have already sung: "Ja, wer auch nur eine Seele" and "Küsse gab sie uns und Reben". These tiny holes in the doily give the words much-needed definition so important in this thickly-textured, fast writing.

The tenor and bass entry at *Andante maestoso* is a classic moment for doing it wrong and compromising intonation and vocal quality, particularly tempting here as it's marked *ff*. It's always a pussycat. Close examination of the full score reveals some wonderful opportunities for contrast in this white-note section. You can shorten "Welt!" by a crotchet/quarter-note in both cases in order to get out of the way of what follows. "Millionen" has dots over the last three notes when the tenors and basses sing it, but not when everyone sings it a few bars later. The tenor/bass "Brüder!" (bar 17) is a pussycat of course, and let's sing it *forte* rather than *fortissimo*; you're not accompanied by many instruments here even if two of them are trombones! *Inalare la voce* will be a huge help in these eight bars. The leap of a seventh at "lieber Vater" for the sopranos will be easiest if they sing a really open vowel on the low note and have a sense that it already contains the high note. The key to high notes is usually in the way we sing the previous note, preparing the space and singing it properly, rather than thinking it's the next note that really matters. "Vater" was *legato* into the short notes on "wohnen" for the tenor/bass statement (bars 23-24), but the rest of the section is long, long, long, open, open, open, with no shortening of the final two syllables.

Adagio ma non troppo, ma divoto only needs to be slightly slower than the previous tempo, and it's essential to check the full score again for *staccato* dots on white notes. The *crescendo* on the first chord only needs to go to *mf* and to make it unanimous let's be precise and aim for that dynamic on the second beat. Even though it's a short note "stürzt" needs to have length and to be *legato* into "nie-der", both of whose syllables are short. "Millionen" should start piano and by picking up the orchestra's *pianissimo* the choir can make a wonderfully effective *crescendo* through "Ahnest du den Schöpfer," to a blazing *fortissimo* on "Welt?". Make sure the tenors are clearly audible at "du den"; nobody else has black notes here. The glottal is expressive at "Such' ihn über'm..." but make sure you don't start the *crescendo* earlier than printed. At the *fortissimo* "Über Sternen" *inalare la voce* will be an enormous help as it will also be in the next five bars of *pianissimo*.

Sopranos and altos can create the feeling of space needed at the top of the voice here, by breathing in on a yawny open throated Ah vowel, before stroking the vowel into that space for the ü. In his wonderfully readable *Conducting Beethoven* Norman Del Mar describes this moment as "conjuring up the whole wide starry heavens on a clear night".

Much of the *Allegro energico, sempre ben marcato* though extremely demanding, takes care of itself. Ironically, once you know what you're doing the same can often be said of difficult music. The two main themes move mainly by step, and despite the fact that they are often high-lying, they are wonderfully singable once you get carried along by Beethoven's extraordinary energy. Energetic choristers will need some reminders though. Before the *fortissimo* climax there are only two *fortissimo* markings: for the basses when they come in before the bar line with the descending main theme (bar 16), and for the altos when they return to their opening theme (bar 38). As usual, beware accents! You will see in the full score that there are fewer of these than have found their way into most vocal scores. In amongst the counterpoint there are for everybody, but in particular the altos (bars 21 and 22), some very tricky bars. These will need careful slow work in order that they become as confident as everything else. Make sure that in this texture of long lines the single cries of "Freude!" can clearly be heard. Sopranos have this first (bars 10 and 12), no problem for them at the top of the texture or the tenors and basses later, but the alto statements can get buried. The key is in opening up the second vowel and not phrasing off. In what can only really be described as the hell-for-leather *fortissimo* bars (bars 64-75), *inalare la voce* is your guide and constant companion, particularly for sopranos on your long top A. It's not as long as it looks of course because it's so fast! At the *subito piano* it's essential that the rhythmic sense doesn't falter even though the bottom has dropped out of the music. Basses shouldn't breathe before the first word, and despite how it's printed, they need to sing "Mi - lli - o - nen". Tenors elide "nest du" and sing "Welt" full length. Altos sing "zelt" full length. The *Tutti* "zelt" four bars later also needs to be full length so there can't be a breath before the *sf* "Brüder!". Don't breathe after "Sternenzelt" eight bars after this (bar 99). If you do, you have no chance of making sense of the composer's *decrescendo* to *piano* in this bar. There is debate over the first alto note five bars before the double bar (bar 104), C or C sharp. You will hear that various great interpreters of Beethoven 9 make different decisions about whether or not to live with the C sharp/natural clash created when the altos sing C sharp. You decide! To me the false relation sounds bizzare and eccentric. So I prefer it!

After the solo quartet has got the *Allegro ma non tanto* started, the chorus come in *piano* and have six bars of unison singing to get to *forte*. It's very effective to get maximum length out of both syllables of "geteilt" (bar 41). And screw your courage to the sticking place over this next entry and don't come in late. Being on time will take care of the *fortissimo*. At *Poco adagio* you can most effectively *decrescendo* on the vowel, so be careful not to arrive early on the n of "Menschen". This is a dramatic tempo change with a much slower crotchet/quarter-note than the previous minim/half-note. The next time it happens (bar 70), leaving the solo quartet *a cappella*, there are alternatives for the chorus. Do they finish at the fast tempo or sing "Menschen" at the new slow speed? There are arguments for both. My own preference is that the chorus finish at the fast tempo thereby getting out of the way at a dramatic mood change. It also means you don't have to worry nearly as much about their intonation or ensemble! In the first *Poco adagio* a decision needs to be made over the soprano ornament (bar 50). Where the soprano soloist has a similar figure in the second *Poco adagio* (bar 73), the ornament is written out. I'm happy for the chorus sopranos to do what she's going to do; it's more interesting and expressive than simply doing exactly what is suggested by the ornament. If Beethoven had wanted that, perhaps he would simply have written it out. And that tends to be my approach to ornaments in general.

The solo quartet have sung their last and we are into the *Prestissimo*. Most conductors will take this faster than the minim/half-note 132, and the unfaltering Norman Del Mar suggests 156. It's *forte* not *fortissimo* and it's crucial to find length in these short notes. It's the kind of moment when I find myself reminding the choir that they should be singing rather than playing the xylophone. Even at this speed some pizza-dough kneading will be helpful. Sing *legato* from the long *inalare la voce* "Welt!" (bar 10) into "Brüder", and don't miss the opportunity for glottal holes in the doily at "muss ein" and "Vater, ein". As earlier, in relatively straightforward music there are very tricky lines which need to be mastered slowly and out of context. In the section starting at bar 30, a breath after every "Welt!" provides welcome relief and contrast with the long phrase starting in bar 43 where "ganzen" is repeated, making that phrase for all voices "der ganzen, ganzen Welt, der ganzen Welt!". The approach to the single statement "Freude!" we adopted before will work again in bar 54, that is, not phrased off, and in order to stop the last syllable of "Götterfunken" getting lost, sing "ken" with the same vowel sound you would use in the English word "enjoy". It goes by too quickly to sound wrong, and it will be heard which a more authentic German vowel won't. Choirs so often sound uncertain in these *Maestoso* bars and often don't move together. This moment needs to be precise and not left to chance. It's a question of arithmetic. Everybody needs to know how many of those little ones make one of those big ones! Check the full score for dynamics again. There's no accent on "schöner" in bar 68. Breathe after the first "Götterfunken!" in bar 69 and don't take the last two notes for granted. They need to be together and remembering the *Prestissimo* tempo from a few bars earlier is the best way to achieve this.

We did it! I like to plant in everyone's imagination the idea of singing in the first performance, and actually the idea that this music was once heard for the first time, obvious I know, but still awe-inspiring, with a composer not knowing how the public would react, and not being able to hear a sound from them when they did.

8

Tips for rehearsing Verdi's *Requiem*

Certain composers, Mahler and Elgar seem most obvious, fill their scores with so many marks of expression that there can seem to be nothing left to add. The Verdi *Requiem*, on the other hand, seems to leave room for interpretation, but there's always the possibility that if the composer hasn't asked for something, he may well not want it. In the end, thank goodness, everyone's ideas will be different. After more than thirty years' experience of this great work, here are mine. Bar numbers correspond with The New Novello Choral Edition.

No.1 Requiem

Musical shaping is to a certain extent instinctive and it can take an effort to suppress that instinct. You will hear some very refined shaping in the opening *Andante*. But it might not be what the composer had in mind. He writes hairpins for the strings but not one for the choir. I think he's clear about what he wants from the choir: *sotto voce, il più piano possibile, sempre **ppp***; as quiet as humanly possible, with an absence of shaping, thereby creating an atmosphere which draws the audience in with its petrified almost inhuman quality. There are plenty of opportunities for exquisite shaping from the chorus in the next seventy minutes but perhaps this is different. Where Verdi asks for *Soli 4 Soprani* let's have four sopranos please(!) and in bars 21/22 remember the words of the great Arturo Toscanini: "Non mangiate le piccole note!" It's the tiny notes, in which we find some length of course, which give these bars their character and *pianissimo* energy.

The pitch is inclined to wobble as the basses come in *forte* at *Poco più*. It's always a pussycat. Though I generally favour breathing with the punctuation allowing transparency in the counterpoint, here I think breaking at the comma after "hymnus" sounds fussy. So let's keep this section really *legato*. Think of the accents on "decet" as lengthenings, and it will help in this section to remember that *forte* means strong rather than loud. In bar 37 the tenors have our first case of *staccato* dots under a phrase mark. Let's decide that the slur means that they are not detached but accented within *piano pianissimo*. There are three pairs of semiquavers/sixteenth-notes in this section, make sure they are all clear. Make sure that bar 50 really is a *subito pianissimo* by not allowing a *diminuendo* in bar 49, and tenors can achieve their accents at "ad te" in forte while still eliding the d and the t. I would clear the chord before the *Attacca subito (come prima)*. It is literally *come prima* until the dotted rhythms of the opening are relaxed at "et lux perpetua luceat eis" and the *crescendo* into *Animando un poco*.

After the soloists have begun the *Animando un poco* (bar 94), both the Ricordi and New

Novello Choral Edition bring the tenors and basses in *pianissimo* and the altos *piano* before the *Tutti fortissimo*. These ATB entry dynamics are too quiet and don't appear in the Eulenberg full score. The tenors and basses are low in their voices here, it's thickly scored and they need to be audible. The *pianissimo* entries that follow can be *legatissimo* providing maximum contrast with the upper strings' *staccato*. As ever with short notes, the choir need to find some length in their semiquavers/sixteenth-notes for "eleison" in bars 107/8. Bars 115-117 are all about the tenors, and the horns of course. There are more tiny accents for the reduced voices in 119/120 and the rest of the movement should take care of itself.

No.2 Dies irae

At the risk of stating the obvious, there is a tendency to oversing at this point. I don't want to spoil anybody's fun so I'm just going to say three things which will make a difference. It's always a pussycat. *Non mangiate le piccole note!* (There aren't many small notes but really deciding to sing the semiquavers/sixteenth-notes in the first two statements suddenly makes it about something other than brute-force). And think of the accents as lengthenings; it will make a huge difference to vocal quality. In bar 38 there has been a fashion for putting the t of "solvet" on the downbeat and breathing before the accented "in". It makes life easier and it's quite effective. But it's not what Verdi wrote. I much prefer to do what's printed with a *crescendo* through the second syllable of "solvet". It's more effective and more Verdi! Accent, accent, accent is what's printed leading into the *a tempo* at bar 45; it's time to think about kneading some pizza-dough and long, long, long!

Bars 54 to 73 give lots of room for interpretation. But beware! It's tempting to shape these two bar phrases as *crescendo/diminuendo* particularly the three marked *cupo*. I've often heard it done like this but I don't find it convincing. What Verdi has written has to be given a chance! It's completely clear, it avoids the obvious, it leads perfectly into the next musical idea and doesn't need enhancement. There is a danger in the fourteen unison *Tutti* bars that come next (bars 78-91) that we won't really be singing at all. It's *piano pianissimo sotto voce* with a very spare orchestral texture of short extremely quiet notes. Do we dare sing! It's all in the score. If we do exactly what's printed the effect will be supremely effective. In rehearsal it's a good idea to sing the first four bars *legato*, singing through all the rests, so that that the unison B flat is really in tune. Then sing it as printed but with a sense of *sostenuto* which will throw it into relief against the accompaniment. And when the notes get longer make sure you stay rhythmically accurate and maintain the *ppp sotto voce* character. The s on "-rus" at *Allegro sostenuto* needs care; the new crotchet/quarter-note is slightly faster than the old minim/half-note.

Most of the time the means of getting the best out of the music essentially stay the same. The fundamentals don't vary. The music is endlessly varied, endlessly fascinating and work of incomprehensible and awesome genius. Even the world's greatest choral director doesn't stand up to comparison with that. So let the music speak for itself. And have the confidence to let it do this by simply applying the handful of ideas, the basic principles, and doing what the composer has asked. Again in the "Tuba mirum" section, finding the length in the short notes and not overdoing the accents will do the trick. This can seem like the opposite of what is on the page. In bar 122 for example, can the semiquavers/sixteenth-notes really be that important? Yes, they can, but even though I've talked about finding length in them they must not become part of the brass triplets. In the following bar a breath at the comma works, but make sure there's some length in the "num"; think of it as a *tenuto* quaver/eighth-note. This section is quite often rescored on the grounds that if it needs to be really loud, why not get the tenors to join the basses and the altos to join the sopranos? I would argue that even at moments like this, and even in the Royal Albert Hall, there is still a degree of subtlety which you lose with the all-hands-on-deck approach. Starting in bar 177 Verdi could hardly have been clearer about how quiet he wants the "Dies irae" contributions from the chorus. Very quiet indeed, though he doesn't go quite as far as he did in *Il Trovatore* where at one point he writes *pppppppppppp*. Count them! 12. Back to the Mezzo-Soprano solo and for all their hardly-dare-utter-a-sound quality these unison statements of "Dies irae!" must be in tune. We can take the *Allegro come prima* "Dies irae!" as read which brings us to the "Rex tremendae". *Non mangiate* ... of course for basses and tenors, and quaver/eighth-note rests with the punctuation after "majestatis!" and "gratis" both times to make space for what comes on the following downbeat. On the three repetitions of "salva" (bars 342-344) it again makes sense to think of the accents as lengthenings and to only sing *forte*; the basses are very much in charge with their *fortissimo*. More *estremamente piano* follows but "salva me" still needs to be sung, and in tune, even if it does give the impression of being whispered. A whisper has no voice and therefore no pitch so it simply can't do the job required here. Singing with a breathy quality, which for all its quietness requires real concentration and physical effort, is what is called for.

And so we go from *estremamente piano* straight to *fortissimo* at the start of twelve bars of *animando* leading to a massive perfect cadence in C. It takes care of itself with perhaps the need to remember the wonderful words of Isobel Baillie: "Never sing louder than lovely!". She prized these words so highly that they became the title of her autobiography. The dust has settled after one of the biggest moments in all music, a universal cry of "salva me", and from the silence a single voice sings those words again, sweetly and unaccompanied. And words I prize highly enough to use as the title of my book come to the rescue of the basses, actually half the basses in bar 372. These four bars are very nerve-wracking in performance. They are so different from what has just happened, and choristers need an utterly reliable way of singing these leads. The stroke, with the lift of the arm as a crotchet/quarter-note upbeat will do the trick. And let's get used to singing these bars from memory, that will make a world of difference particularly as there's *animando un poco* to negotiate. There's a change of direction in the next return of the "Dies irae" but it doesn't really present any problems. Make sure the tuning of unisons is absolutely spot-on from bar 601 to 603.

The *Largo* Lacrymosa section provides soloists and chorus with some of the most singable music ever written. If it ain't broke don't fix it and by the same token, if it's easy let's not look for problems. We've seen *staccato* dots under a slur but we really do have detached notes in this section; first of all for the divided sopranos in bar 642; let's think of them as quavers/eighth-notes but *tenuto* to make them more expressive, and for everyone on "ergo" and/or "Deus" at the *animando un poco* (bars 657-660), let's just find a sliver of daylight between these *staccato* notes. If ever there were a moment showing why superstar soloists need experience and expertise as ensemble singers the twelve bar section starting in bar 666 is it. Let's just say it can be absolutely exquisite but sometimes it isn't.

Back to us! Look at the rising phrase the first basses, tenors and sopranos have in common in bars 677 and 678. It's often worth taking a moment like this and rehearsing it in unison to make sure intonation and quality really match. Here it will be a good idea to practise it stopping on and sustaining the D flat as that's always a hard note to tune in the soprano voice. The descending phrase in bar 61 is detached *staccato*. I always enjoyed the contrast provided by the fact that in the Ricordi edition the tenors and basses *staccato* didn't continue into the second bar. I was disappointed to find that this is not consistent with the full score and that it's been changed in the New Novello Choral Edition. Make your own mind up; I might stick to the old way and pretend I haven't noticed. Only one more comment on this mighty movement: don't underestimate the Amen. It's only two bars, but it's a long phrase needing a good breath, good posture and complete dynamic control.

No.4 Sanctus
Here it is! That C for Choir 1 basses may well be the reason for this whole book. And if you don't believe me, listen to recording after recording after recording. I can't claim to have listened to them all, but time after time I have heard this note hit, assaulted, abused. That's no way to treat a pussycat! It's *forte* not *fortissimo*. And there's another staffing issue here. Should the tenors and the Choir 2 basses really be standing idle? Yes they should. The choir hasn't been singing for a whole movement and Verdi reintroduces them with a degree of subtlety. It's a loud start but the point is that the three statements of "Sanctus" get progressively louder. Also, for the first time in the work we have double choir. If we use a double choir layout we can get a sense of antiphonal singing in this opening and later in the second *Allegro* section from bar 79. This is the only double choir movement in the work. Should we bother with double choir formation? I believe we should, as just a glance at these pages makes it very clear that this was intended. The same question presents itself in *The Dream of Gerontius*. There are only about twenty pages of double choir in a vocal score of nearly 180 pages but again, the effect the composer intends at this point depends on it.

As the opening eight bars and the next section are both marked *Allegro* it's very easy to take the second *Allegro* simply at twice the speed of the opening eight bars. But it's not what the metronome mark indicates. The fugal section is quite a lot slower. And the orchestra, with their *staccato* quavers/eighth-notes need it to be slower. You want a fast fugue? It's ok, you're getting one later! Once we've got off on the right foot, that is at the right speed, this music looks after itself. There's plenty of detail to get right, the dynamic scheme and use of offbeat accents in the fourth bar of the subject and third bar of the countersubject for example, but it's all gloriously singable and full of contrast. I remember once hearing the strings rehearse part of this movement. That sounds lovely I thought, but why aren't they rehearsing the Verdi *Requiem*? They were playing music I had never been aware of. Unless this movement is really carefully balanced a lot of people are going to a lot of trouble for nothing.

No.5 Agnus Dei

Again I'm hoping that the soloists are experienced and sensitive ensemble singers. I remember a time when I felt disappointed even let down by a composer writing a unison tune. Could he not have made more of an effort? Latterly I'm happy to say that I find perfectly in tune unison singing enormously satisfying. In bars 14 to 26 we get help with the intonation as we are supported by the orchestra, but it's a good idea to rehearse this *a cappella* and to tell the choir when they first sing it with the orchestra that if they can't hear the orchestra they're singing too loudly. A reminder about posture will help the intonation, and make sure nobody goes digging for the bottom G in bar 20. In bars 40-45 the sopranos and altos will need to rehearse by themselves *a cappella* to get their unison in tune. You needn't insist on *pianissimo* until it's in tune. One thing at a time! And on the last page tenors and basses will need care and attention for their solo lines. Again, don't start rehearsing it too quietly, and concentrate on open-throated *legato*. A bad habit will probably rear its ugly head here: a tendency to hum an n before the d of "dona". I frequently have to deal with this and every time I do, half the choir look at me as if to say I'm glad you're dealing with that.

No.7 Libera me

Even in the great concert halls with the greatest singers things go wrong. I won't name either soprano soloist or conductor but a very distinguished soprano indeed took part in a performance of this and perhaps her jet-setting lifestyle caught up with her as her three colleagues sang their wonderful "Lux aeterna". She fell asleep. Having been woken up by the distinguished maestro and having got to her feet, she realised that she had no idea what note to start on. She picked a note and began reciting. The fact that it was the wrong note didn't matter until the orchestra came in and then it really did matter. She took a while to find her bearings. A shame, but only a moment in a brilliant career. The *senza misura* bars are a real ensemble exercise and it's a good idea for the choir to get used to them unconducted. No syllables should be stressed and the second statement needs to be appreciably quieter than the first.

In this final reprise of the "Dies irae" we sing words and music that we haven't sung before, so there are new opportunities! I had a piano teacher once who talked about "emphatic offs" meaning lifting the fingers off the keys exactly when asked to and I'm always talking about how important the rests are. From bar 76 three consecutive two bar phrases finish with a quaver/eighth-note not a crotchet/quarter-note. The difference is night and day! And in "miseriae" which comes twice, the energy is in the "-ri-". The choir has shown so much contrast and colour in this work so far but from bar 132 we finally get the chance to sing *ppp a cappella*. It's challenging of course but we have the means. Not slowing down will immediately make life easier and when singing this quietly *inalare la voce* will give a sense of dynamism and direction. A composer will often write a *crescendo* followed by a *diminuendo* without an arrival dynamic in the middle. I usually decide on one if only in order to be ready for the question when it comes. So, for the downbeat of bar 136 I might decide that we should have got as far as *piano*. Verdi's use of hairpins is interesting in the next three bars. Sopranos have the shaping we might expect on "dona" but everyone else has the opposite. It is a challenge to go the opposite way and will need close attention. It is so important in music in Latin not to cling on to what we think of as the correct word stress but to see how the composer has responded to the ancient language. It's safe to assume that in the *Requiem* and his other great Latin work *Quattro Pezzi Sacri* (three of which are in Latin), Verdi felt he had something new to say, and that sometimes that was going to involve deliberately contradicting the speech rhythms that he had known all his life. So when Verdi, Stravinsky and Poulenc for example seem to be flying in the face of Catholic tradition, go with them! In this slow and quiet music intonation is of course a challenge. Remember that gravity will pull the pitch down so staying tall and keeping the throat open will be essential. This section is also an object lesson in the difference between descending and ascending intervals: descending ones are small and ascending ones are big. So, in bars 141-143 sopranos have a tiny downward step but a bigger step back, and basses have two big jumps to a G flat followed by what feels like a really big jump to the G natural. The language can sound naïve and illogical in our line of work but these ideas are our bread and butter. These principles of intonation will help to get bar 160 in tune and you definitely need a dynamic ready for the downbeat of bar 164; *forte* might seem a bit much so I keep p*oco forte* up my sleeve for moments like this.

The *Allegro risoluto* is in fact only slightly faster than the Sanctus fugue but there is a lot more detail to master. Having said that Verdi is not as exacting as Mahler or Elgar when it comes to marks of expression, he has gone to a great deal of trouble here and the subject comes in every conceivable guise, the articulation varying even between each voice's first entry. Make sure you pay close attention to the full score to find out exactly what's required. It has become customary to modify the fugue subject by turning the tied crotchet/quarter-note on "aeterna" into a rest. I can see the arguments for doing this and there is a comma, but it is a significant departure from what Verdi wrote. Surely the approach should always be to try to make sense of what the composer has written before making changes. So the question you could be asking is "what are we doing wrong that doesn't allow what the composer has written to work?". Here it could well be that everyone is simply singing too loudly. The first syllable of "tremenda" is the key to the power of the word, so find some length in it even if it is tucked in the far right hand corner of the last beat in the bar; it's yet another little note that mustn't be eaten! Verdi's endless inventiveness with marks of expression in this section requires real vigilance and good eyesight! It's so easy for something to get lost or forgotten. For example, in the section where the soloist joins (bars 262-273), there are accents for the basses in "Libera" and "Domine" on the most unlikely syllables. They need to be heard and they stop the music sounding too comfortable at this exquisite moment. It's almost as if the basses are warning the soprano soloist that it's not that simple. Sopranos can modify their vowel to Ah for their ascent to the high B in bar 292. There are *staccato* dots under slurs and *staccato* dots without slurs; they need different treatment, the latter being detached wherever they occur, for example from the second half of everyone's first bar in the *piano* section that begins in bar 312. I won't dare come between you and the great climax to this section, but let me just point out one more syllable before I leave you to the work's devastating conclusion. You can make something special happen by finding length in the first syllable of "tremenda" in bar 397; it's your last chance and a unique moment.

9

Tips for preparing Brahms's *Ein deutsches Requiem*

Though always performed now in the seven movement version premiered in Leipzig in 1869, I do feel that the version heard in Bremen the previous year had its advantages. On that occasion only six movements were heard, the soprano solo movement had not yet been written, and the movements by Brahms were interleaved with music by other composers including "I know that my Redeemer liveth" from *Messiah*. In the Bremen version therefore, the choir got some time off! There is always a sense for me that the choir, having sung the hugely demanding second movement, should get some recovery time before embarking on another long and demanding movement. But history has outvoted me! Simon Halsey once suggested that the gaps be opened up again and filled with music specially commissioned. Jonathan Dove was the composer he had in mind. I like that idea. I also like the idea of reconstructing the Bremen premiere with its interpolations by Bach, Handel and Schumann; but I might let somebody else approach the orchestral librarian.

No.1 Selig sind, die da Leid tragen

These opening three bars can of course be sung from memory. Even though there is no *crescendo*, there needs to be some sense of energy, which *inalare la voce* can provide. I might turn the tables on the choir and get them to conduct me. Getting them all to conduct in 4/4 with a rhythmic upbeat and a pussycat downbeat will do wonders for their sense of ensemble and unanimity of feel. Look carefully at the *crescendo* in bars 24/25: the top of the phrase is the beginning of the soprano "werden" not the middle syllable of "getröstet". It's so much more interesting! In bars 29 and 31 we need to have answers to questions about the hairpins. A small *crescendo* to the second beat, followed by a *diminuendo* is all that's required. This movement provides wonderful opportunities for *legato* singing on the ideal vowels for example in bars 35/36. It will help the sopranos on "Tränen" in bars 52-54 to remember that the first vowel involves all the Ah space with a minor modification of the shape. The "werden mit Freuden" leads for all voices in bars 55-58 need the *legato sostenuto* approach. It's easy just to start playing the xylophone here in this syllabic music, but you will achieve a much more effective *forte* if you find the length in every note. The more I look at it, the more this movement seems to be an object lesson in alternating *legato sostenuto* in syllabic passages, and open-throated *legato* in melismas. Look at the soprano line in bars 72-74: it could be a line from a song by Richard Strauss, and it needs the same approach. Be relentless in your pursuit of *legato* singing! Once the *legato* is right, and has been achieved with a real sense of trombone-slide connection between notes, an open throat and a free jaw, the sound is transformed. To elide or not to elide? In slow music like this, there's time to sing both final and initial consonants and it can be expressive, for example in "Leid tragen" and "mit Tränen" so I would recommend it. When singing in German a decision needs to be made about what to do with the Schwa vowel, denoted by the IPA symbol ə. This unstressed vowel, the second vowel in "tragen", "sollen" and "werden", finds its English equivalent in the first syllable of "about". You cannot sing on this vowel, short notes in particular get lost altogether, think of the *Prestissimo* in Beethoven 9: "Seid umschlungen, Millionen, diesen Kuss der ganzen Welt". Those unstressed syllables need all the help they can get; and the Schwa sounds very unbeautiful on a long note such as the sopranos have in "tragen" in bar 22. As previously, I recommend the sound found in "enjoy". It can feel very open and brash, but it's a sound that carries, it's a sound where you can find the uniformity crucial for good intonation, and from the auditorium it sounds right. I've heard British choirs try to sing an authentic German Amen. If you hear the Germans say this word in church, you will notice that there's barely any second syllable at all. You can't sing that, and in my experience, German choirs are happy to sing the singable but inauthentic version. Just two more comments on this opening movement: get sopranos and tenors to rehearse their "getröstet werden" leads in bars 144-148 together in unison; and make sure the black notes are long, *legato sostenuto ma pianissimo* in bars 154/155. You might need some pizza-dough!

No.2 Denn alles Fleisch es ist wie Gras

We saw in the Beethoven 9 chapter that the glottal stop or Knacklaut in German is a major factor in the authentic sung language. It is certainly important in creating the right effect both in these opening bars and in the *forte* version after one of the greatest *crescendi* ever composed. In the *piano* version altos and basses must resist the temptation to dig or push. The tenors are in a more favourable part of their range and if the choir can't be heard the orchestra is too loud. In the *forte* section the *diminuendo* that begins in bar 60 must begin *forte*; it's so easy to have let the dynamic relax after the breath in bar 58. It's too obvious and not what's printed. There's a danger at both *piano* and *forte* that we don't commit to the full length of the vowels in "alles", "Fleisch", "ist", in fact all the white notes. Consonants need to be as late as you dare and not exaggerated. In the diphthong "Fleisch" ninety-nine percent of the vowel is Ah. Make sure you have seen exactly what the hairpins indicate in bars 69-72; the top of the phrase is a bar later than you might have thought.

In the *Etwas bewegter* section on the 1947 recording of this work conducted by Herbert von Karajan, you can hear the soprano soloist Elisabeth Schwarzkopf singing with the chorus sopranos. She contributes some wonderful *legato* singing, in particular to the downward fourth in bar 80 and to "Erde" in bars 101-103. Now that's what I call *legato*! How wonderful that she had volunteered to sing with the sopranos to keep them in tune. It's tempting to sing too loud at "Aber des Herrn Wort" at bar 198. It's only *forte* and it's always a pussycat, though I admit that the last-beat-in-the-bar pussycat is something of a rarity. A *crescendo* on the first vowel here can be extremely effective. The bass part at the beginning of the *Allegro non troppo* is angular and unpredictable. It should be memorised and a lot of care taken that none of the quavers/eighth-notes gets lost. The challenge with "Freude" from bar 219 is familiar from Beethoven 9. Make sure that the second syllable doesn't get lost by opening up the vowel, singing the black note full length, and not phrasing off; the downward intervals take care of the phrasing. At bar 225 the first note needs to be full length and *fortissimo*. It's so easy to *decrescendo* through bar 224, but then there's no chance of achieving what needs to be *piano subito*. In bars 238/9 I love the fact that "und Schmerz" is *piano* with no hairpins; it allows maximum contrast with the shapely "und Seufzen". In bar 252 one frequently hears beats three and four shortened. I much prefer to interpret what is printed as only shortening "er-" and therefore singing "sie er-" *legato*, with a Knacklaut of course. We will be revisiting this idea in Movement 6. In the *Tranquillo*, starting in bar 303, I would avoid any overworking of "Freude", rather, take the fact that there is neither a *crescendo* through "ewige" nor a *diminuendo* through "Freude" to signify that that isn't what Brahms wanted. And that fits perfectly with the *Tranquillo* feel. All of the technical demands in the last twenty bars benefit from *inalare la voce*: high quiet singing for the sopranos, a long slow *crescendo*, a long sustained *forte* and a long slow *diminuendo*. Happy Seals was invented for music like this!

No.3 Herr, lehre doch mich
In German, as in English, the terminal r is a moot point. Fashion changes, but pronouncing the terminal r when singing either of these languages at the moment is definitely out of fashion. However, I do like to hear a rolled r when a German word ends in a double r. And that in-tune, voiced rolled r, combined with the Knacklaut in the chorus's opening bars, and the printed dynamics, will achieve exactly the desired effect. As in Beethoven 9 the chorus gets the chance to emulate the baritone soloist, but here we're asked to go further. Our "vor dir" in bars 53-54 has a *crescendo*. Let's make sure it is a *crescendo* rather than just an accent on "dir". A *crescendo* through "ist" in bars 61/62 is also highly effective. The passage beginning in bar 144 is demanding in terms of range and has big intervals. It needs thorough preparation. It's easy for the tenors to be wrong-footed in bar 150, where they come in on the second beat, as the sopranos do in bar 152. Sopranos and tenors need to handle bar 155 correctly. They might think it's all about the top A. It is. But you sing a great top A by preparing properly, which means finding length and openness on the D, and making sure it already belongs to the A. In bars 159-161 "wes soll ich mich trösten?" has unmistakably the feel of the *pianissimo* "über Sternen muß er wohnen" from Beethoven 9, but fortunately it's not as high or as quiet!

There's no question over the demanding nature of the fugal conclusion to this movement. For a start, the fugue subject has a range of an octave and a fourth! But it's so rewarding, and you wouldn't want to be stuck on the same note for thirty-six bars like several of your orchestral colleagues. Tenors lead the way. Bottle of Raspberry Tizer please! would be a good start as there's a big temptation to follow this melodic shape up, down and then up again. In fact, it's a wonderfully singable line often moving by step and manageable in one breath; you may need to stop people shortening "Hand"

and snatching a quick breath. As ever, the *legato sostenuto* approach and staying tall and open will get the best results. Even in a texture as dense as this anything that isn't *legato* sticks out. So, tenors need to be beautifully *legato* on the notes of the A major *arpeggio* in bars 179 and 184. And of course, the more dense the texture the more important the holes in the doily. These are provided by the commas, in particular the one after "an" making that note a quaver/eighth-note followed by a quaver/eighth-note breath, and after "Qual" in the last six bars. The figure that the sopranos have in bar 185 and tenors in 202 needs not to be worked too hard. It's doubled by instruments in both places and can be sung *leggiero*, actually recalling the feel of our flexibility exercise, the Messy scale. And, finally, the dynamics need to be calibrated at the end in such a way that a *crescendo* is still possible.

No.4 Wie lieblich sind deine Wohnungen

For many, including me, this was not only our first experience of *Ein deutsches Requiem* but also our first experience of Brahms. I'm reminded by it of Charles Villiers Stanford's attitude to "And the glory of the Lord" from *Messiah*; at about five minutes long, it's a perfect miniature in every respect. My first instinct is not to try too hard and to let the music speak for itself. There are moments of Beethovenian struggle in *Ein deutsches Requiem* but here's the complete opposite. To elide or not to elide at "sind deine"? This is medium-paced music so there's still time for both final and initial consonants and I would recommend singing them both. But don't make a meal of it, particularly in the tenor solo line. The tenors' "Zebaoth" in bars 9/10 has bigger intervals than anyone else's; as in the previous movement it will stick out of the texture unless it's really *legato*, and the success of bars 40-43 is all about the tenors. In the *crescendo* leading to the first climax at bar 56, it's important to involve the upbeats. A version with big downbeats seems to me much less convincing than a version where you find length and quality in the upbeats "ver-" and "und", while still allowing "sehnet" to phrase off naturally with its falling interval. And beware the big downbeat in bars 66-69. The strings have *fp* in all of these bars, but apart from the violas, who sustain the lowest notes of each chord, their music is totally different and complementary to what the voices are doing. There's no need to borrow their accents. The section beginning with the upbeat to bar 124 "die loben dich immerdar" is also all about contrasting and complementary articulation. The lower strings have separate bows, upper strings have *staccato* quavers/eighth-notes and the singers are in their natural habitat, praising God evermore *legato sostenuto*. Sopranos and tenors might prefer to elide at the top of their ranges in bars 168-169 with alto and basses to match; the words have been heard clearly plenty of times by now. That will do for this movement. As previously, in the spirit of 'if it ain't broke don't fix it', let's not look for problems where there may well not be any.

No.5 Ihr habt nun Traurigkeit

Possibly the best thing that can happen in this movement is that the choir be barely noticed. If the choir is to be noticed, let it be for its *piano mezza voce* and *pianissimo* singing; let it be for its *legato* singing in bar 19 and in the pairs of quavers/eighth-notes in for example bars 35 and 36 (that's not Baroque phrasing!), and for the tenors' *legato* in bars 63/64. Let it be for the shaping of bar 70, long, long, long, long through the *crescendo* even though they look short. Nobody will notice the choir's *diminuendo* in their last bar but let's do it anyway!

No.6 Denn wir haben hie keine bleibende Statt

There are essentially two approaches to the opening choral music here, both at the start and in the contrapuntal version starting in bar 18. Some interpreters take their lead from the *pizzicato* lower strings and add accents to the crotchets/quarter-notes while some follow the *legato arco* of the upper strings. I would argue that with the strings patting their heads and rubbing their tummies at the same time the choir doesn't have to, and that if the choir isn't too loud the *pizzicato* strings will actually lend just the right degree of accentuation to their *legato piano*. In the *Vivace* I reconsider my approach to elision. It's fast, but there is time for both consonants at "wird die" and I like its energy. In this glorious music, here and in the section starting in bar 127, maximum contrast between *staccato* and *molto legato* (not printed) is crucial. In most cases it's obvious what to do, for example the difference in articulation between bars 145-146 and 147-149. (Don't be misled by the *staccato* in the piano reduction; it refers to the strings who continue *staccato* while most of the woodwind and brass like the voices change to *legato*.) The *staccato* dot sometimes tempts the performer to isolate the note with the dot regardless of what has happened immediately before. So, for example the last notes of bars 165 and 174 are often short. There is a comma after "Hölle" but on this occasion I wouldn't recommend a hole in the doily; it's much more effective to sing *legato* into the *staccato* "wo". And notice that "Sieg" is short in bar 167 but long in bar 178. The fugal *Allegro* that concludes this movement is extraordinarily rich in texture and contrast. Use of the glottal in the subject at "und Ehre und Kraft" will add character to the *legato sostenuto*. The counter-subject can have a *leggiero* feel whilst still being *legato* and on the other rare occasions when Brahms has written crotchets/quarter-notes, for example for the sopranos in bar 242, they need to be nimble. Some conductors take this *Allegro* in four. It's not what is indicated and makes life rather hard work for everybody. It's so important to find lightness of touch in music that looks as massive as this. Singing *forte* rather than *fortissimo* is crucial of course and it means that everyone has something more to give on the two occasions when *fortissimo* is indicated. Conducting in two enables you to go into four when you want to take your time, for example going into the two *fortissimo* bars, 289 and 315, and in the closing bars.

No.7 Selig sind die Toten

Everybody apart from the altos has this opening theme. It makes sense to rehearse the sopranos and tenors in unison as the tenors' lead in bar 103 is identical to this soprano opening. *Inalare la voce* for quality on the opening note. It begins *forte* and doesn't need to get louder but the whizzing finger will give it a sense of direction. I recommend elision in "von nun", a hole in the doily after "an" and a real sense of length on each of the notes of the triplet. Despite a feeling of calm these opening twenty-eight bars do need to be sung *forte* in order to contrast with all the *piano* singing later in the movement. I would make beat 2 the top of a small *crescendo* in bar 41. In German the final s is never voiced and an s before a vowel is always voiced. So, in bar 43, "daß sie", there are two different s sounds and sounding them both gives the bar just enough rhythmic energy. There are so many opportunities in this movement for *legato* singing sometimes on pairs of notes and sometimes over a longer phrase. How can we satisfy Brahms's demand for *dolce* in bar 66? Well, for the sopranos and tenors *legato* is a good start. Do I give the impression of being obsessed with *legato*? I am. It's the same as a chef being obsessed with seasoning. And remember: *chi non lega, non canta*! Attention to the printed dynamics and the relentless quest for *legato* are all you need for the remainder of this movement. And for the sopranos in bar 158 a sense of contrary motion will help as you approach the A from the F. The jaw free, the throat open, a sopranino trombone-slide *legato*, think Elisabeth Schwarzkopf, and a feeling that the space you need for the A is lower than the space you have on the F, and that the going up is counter-weighted in the imagination by something going down.

10

Tips for preparing Mendelssohn's *Elijah*

No.1 Help, Lord!
Letters in this chapter refer to Edition Eulenberg 6404. We know each other pretty well now, so much of what I have to say will be familiar. There's a big and often irresistible temptation to oversing these opening bars. You're desperate, cold and hungry, and the orchestral *crescendo* before the chorus's first exclamation, added to the adrenaline of the moment, could tip you over the edge. But it really is always a pussycat, and the right approach to these cries for help will keep them in tune, guarantee their quality and increase their potency.

The getting-out-of-the-way hole in the doily is really important in *Elijah* and there are two of these on the first page. I recommend shortening "Lord!" in the fifth bar and "us?" two bars later; both become a dotted crotchet/quarter-note. It adds clarity which will be desirable particularly in a resonant building. In an attempt to be expressive we might tend to overpronounce "The harvest now is over, the summer days are gone; and yet no power cometh to help us;". It's even more of a danger in the choral recitative at the end of this movement. In the *Messiah* chapter I talked about keeping a small mouth in order to maintain a *legato* feel at "and their words unto the ends of the world" in "Their sound is gone out". But even more helpful is an idea I got from Edward Brooks, a singing teacher at the Royal College of Music. He maintained that you should always be whispering the words. Try whispering "the infant children ask for bread;". That is as hard as your mouth needs to work. Now sing it with that in mind. Beautifully *legato* and crystal clear, even when you elide "infant children".

Holes in the doily are an exception to my rule of trying to do what's printed. I like to find out what happens when we take a composer's directions literally, and don't allow ourselves to do what is natural and obvious. Here's a good example: the first statement of "Will then the Lord be no more God in Zion?" doesn't have a *crescendo*. The next statement does have a *crescendo*, which I would allow to contradict the customary stress in the word "Zion". And make sure a big downbeat is avoided on all of these statements of "Zion"; the cumulative effect of these phrases certainly won't benefit from that. On the first of many occasions in *Elijah*, there can be a sense in this movement that the choir's *legato sostenuto* approach complements the separate bows and generally more detached playing of the orchestra. I'd like to see, or perhaps just hear, the kneading of pizza-dough in the last four bars before the recitative, and let's not make that *diminuendo* before it's printed; a descending passage is getting quieter anyway.

No.5 Yet doth the Lord see it not
How appropriate is it for the chorus to adopt a mocking tone in this movement? I've heard that approach, but for me the point is that The People are not doing the mocking. It is their perception that they are being mocked and cursed. So, rather than shortening and accenting the crotchets/quarter-notes in bar five I suggest that a *legato sostenuto* approach works better to express their sense of being oppressed. *Legato sostenuto?* Again? This chorus master really is obsessed with *legato sostenuto*! Won't everything end up sounding the same? No, because the music is inexhaustibly rich and various. If this commitment to *legato sostenuto* must be described as an obsession, then think of it in the same terms as a gardener's obsession with watering or a baker's obsession with yeast. It's essential.

It's hard to make the notes in the first bar really speak. They need length of course. I think we need the t on "Yet" though we can elide the two th sounds; "see it" needs a glottal in order to be clear, and make sure there's some length in "it". The angular curse motif first sung by the sopranos doesn't need to be accented, first and second violins are taking care of the accents. And the energy of the string articulation at "his wrath will pursue us" means the choir can concentrate on smoothness and quality while still being sensitive to the meaning.

No.9 Blessed are the men who fear him
Such wonderfully singable music! Let's have holes in the doily after "peace". At the soprano/tenor handover this gives just the right degree of transparency, it also works well after the *Tutti* statement at B, even though all you are getting out of the way of, by making that minim/half note a dotted crotchet/quarter note, is the third beat of the bar. There are precious few printed rests in this movement in the *Tutti* passages, but applying the doily principle at punctuation marks will work perfectly well. Once again you add refinement by shortening "peace" seven bars before the end, and by separating the last three statements of "Blessed" with quaver/eighth-note rests after perfectly in-tune voiced final consonants.

No.16 O Thou, who makest thine Angels, Spirits
Non mangiate le piccole note! gets you a long way with "The fire descends from heav'n!" followed by a commitment to *legato* for "The flames consume his off'ring" contrasting with the furious string figuration. Unison octaves suit the drama of the moment perfectly at the choral "Take all the prophets of Baal." Time spent getting this perfectly in tune will not be wasted.

No.20 Thanks be to God
To a certain extent Mendelssohn modelled *Elijah* on Handel's *Israel in Egypt*, that's why it doesn't begin with an overture, and we seem only a short step away from Handel in this chorus at A. A few observations can make a difference, usually concerning little notes with potential energy that can nevertheless go for nothing. The key, as ever, is to find length. "The waters gather, they rush along!"; "their fury is mighty"; "But the

Lord is above them, <u>and</u> Al-mighty!"; these two syllables, low in the voices every time, can be really effective and should be preceded by a quaver/eighth-note rest. Do you remember the bass I referred to in an earlier chapter who asked "Is it still a pussycat?". He was asking about a "Hallelujah" starting on a top E flat in Mendelssohn's *Lobgesang*. He could just as easily have been asking about the final *fortissimo* unison statement of "Thanks be to God!". You know the answer.

No.22 Be not afraid

The sopranos' first four notes need to contain the upcoming top G; in other words they need to be sung in a way that makes the G easy. So, have that note in mind from the start and don't descend with the *arpeggio*, stay poised. The low E can be sung very lightly as the altos are singing it too. At A, "thy" needs all the length the basses, altos and tenors can find to make it audible. In the same way, at *Più animato* the first word of "Though thousands languish" is low and short and needs all the length you can muster for it to make any impression. My distinguished colleague Adrian Partington has pointed out that the "it" in "yet it shall not come nigh thee" doesn't actually refer to anything because Mendelssohn only sets a single verse from Psalm 91. Incidentally, he also raises a very valid question about the closing words of "Surely He hath borne our griefs": what exactly does "the chastisement of our peace was upon him" mean?

No.24 Woe to him!

There are excellent examples in this chorus of how energy is contained in short notes, and of how orchestral and choral articulation can be completely different but entirely complementary. Energy in the small notes is not a new idea of course, but here we see how transforming it can be to overall effectiveness even when that energy involves unimportant words and unobvious points in the bar: "he closed <u>the</u> heavens" and "spoken <u>in the</u> name of the Lord?".

Four bars before C some vocal scores have *staccato* dots in the piano reduction. Don't be misled. The dots shouldn't really be there as in the full score you will only find *staccato* in the lower strings. The effect Mendelssohn is aiming for here and two bars later, relies entirely on the contrast of short notes from the orchestra and longer notes from the choir. Any homogenising of orchestral and choral articulation at moments like this flies in the face of the composer's meticulously considered intentions. He knows best. And incidentally, piano reductions, though much more carefully rendered than they were in the nineteenth century, still contain occasional red herrings. At the end of the movement the drama can be intensified by doily holes after "So go ye forth" and "seize on him!" and by finding length in "shall", one of those unlikeliest-moment-in-the-bar opportunities.

No.29 He, watching over Israel

More gloriously singable music! By now you just need to be left alone to enjoy yourself. My only comment relates to the dynamics: take them literally and interesting things happen. For example, the descending phrase four bars before C is not the *diminuendo*; it starts in the next bar with the sopranos and subsequently the other voices coming in *forte*. Nearly every *diminuendo* in this movement is from *forte* and it's not a bad idea to write *f* over *dim*. In this supremely sophisticated music this attention to detail is not just the icing on the cake; rather, it's recognising and respecting the trouble the composer has gone to, and allowing it to pay dividends.

No.34 Behold, God the Lord passed by

Shall we dare to do what the composer has asked at "And a mighty wind"? He hasn't written any accents over the voice parts. The upper strings' quavers/eighth-notes will provide the accentuation unaided if you let them, and the words, as ever, need only be whispered. Make sure "wind" and "-round" are no longer than the printed length. This E minor section can be taut and dramatic without any sense of melodrama; you just need to have the courage to do as the composer asks, no more, no less. After the double bar at H you will frequently hear a completely new tempo. Why? Everything changes after the double bar: key, dynamic, mood, but the tempo doesn't need to, and nothing in the score suggests that it should. Mendelssohn used *Più animato* in No.22 so presumably he would have used some Italian words here if he had wanted a new speed. So, the speed remains constant, and if that doesn't seem to work it's almost certainly because the first section has been taken faster than the metronome mark. Nearly every note left in this movement is a white one, but there is juice in the black ones even though, once again, they are always the last beat of the bar and never on interesting words.

No. 38 Then did Elijah

I'm almost done with talking about little notes. At least I'm in good company: Toscanini and Wagner for a start. And I hate missed opportunities which is why I'm going to mention "He stood <u>on the</u> mount of Sinai, <u>and</u> heard the judgements <u>of the</u> future," and seven bars later "<u>and in</u> Horeb, <u>its</u> vengeance." And, recalling *Israel in Egypt* again, "Lo! there came a fi-<u>ery</u> chariot, with fi-<u>ery</u>, fi-<u>ery</u> horses; <u>and he</u>...". This style of singing is in complete contrast to the *legato sostenuto* required for "went by a whirlwind to heaven:" which need not be accented; three trombones and an ophicleide are on the case!

No.42 And then shall your light break forth

Let's have a hole in the doily at the comma in the opening phrase and length in "your". The Ah vowel makes "light" a wonderful word to sing on but in terms of energy it's the last note of that bar that needs attention with as much length as you can find in "break". At *Allegro. Doppio movimento* a *leggiero* feel will prevent these final pages becoming too monumental, and a hole in the doily at the comma after "Creator" will add elegance. Don't let the *leggiero* feel make "how excellent thy name" bounce. There's no contradiction here, it's *leggiero ma legato sostenuto*. And remember: *chi non lega, non canta!*

11

Not conducting *O clap your hands* by Orlando Gibbons

When the great Belgian conductor Philippe Herreweghe told me that he didn't know any music by Orlando Gibbons, it was this work along with the verse anthem *This is the record of John* that immediately came to mind as the perfect place to start. But how will going back to a five-minute *a cappella* work by an English composer from the first quarter of the seventeenth century feel after Beethoven, Brahms, Verdi and Mendelssohn? On its own terms this English anthem can stand comparison with anything, and in a dystopian future where funding for the arts has dwindled even further, making the mounting of performances of nineteenth century Requiems and oratorios unthinkable, we will at least have treasures like this to perform with a few friends in our methane-from-landfill powered living pods.

I'm working with the edition by John Morehen published by OUP in *The Oxford Book of Tudor Anthems*. The score has been assembled principally from a set of hand-written part-books in York Minster Library dating from about 1675. Editors like John Morehen and latterly my former tutor John Milsom have made the repertoire from this period easily accessible to modern choirs, sometimes, though not in this case, even composing a part where a particular part-book has been lost. But these editors, who have had to make certain decisions, would never claim to have had the last word, and uniquely amongst the works discussed in this book, there is freedom here to make our own decisions about phrasing, dynamics and even pitch.

Despite its SSAATTBB page-layout (an editorial decision) this is a double-choir work, and a concert performance should position the choirs accordingly. Having said that, there's far more eight-part counterpoint in these 133 bars than you would find in most eight-part works, even, dare I say it, those by JS Bach. As with most double-choir works the canonic nature of much of the writing means there is no sense of 'firsts' and 'seconds'; the ranges of Soprano 1 and 2, for example are the same. Nevertheless the conductor will always be approached by a second soprano trying to excuse herself from Soprano 1. In fact, none of the parts is high and in some cases I would do this piece a semitone higher than printed.

Very occasionally I attend concerts of *a cappella* music where, for at least one piece, the conductor lets the choir perform unconducted. I am inclined to adopt that approach here. Having taken rehearsals and made decisions about dynamics and articulation there will come a point when I should have made myself redundant, a moment when all the elements for a first-class performance are in place and it's time to hand over. Ironically, I'm handing over not because there's nothing left to do but because there's still too much to do, too many leads to give and simply too many opportunities get in the way. So even though it's a staple of the Anglican choral repertoire, in a concert I believe it needs to be treated like a sacred madrigal.

That madrigalian feeling surely needs to start with a sense of two in a bar rather four, that the downbeat is light and that there's a *leggiero* feel at the same time as a sense of *legato sostenuto*. I would also recommend the subtlest underlining of "clap" in this opening section. Whilst it doesn't need to be loud, these opening bars need conviction. I've been cautious about using *mezzo forte* ever since I heard that Shostakovich had coined the word *mezzofortist* to describe second-rate musicians, so for these opening bars I may well use *poco forte*; it will naturally have risen to *forte* by bar 5, the first moment where everyone is singing.

In an eight-part piece it's more important than ever that there's transparency in the texture, and the doily principle, letting the light shine through by breathing with the punctuation, should certainly guide us here. There's no need to breathe or break at every single comma; singing through the commas after "together" for Tenor 1 in bar 2 and Soprano 1 in bar 3 makes sense, but there could be a moment of daylight at the end of bar 4, a tiny silence for everyone apart from Tenor 2. Unanimity of feel at moments like this is what ensemble singing is all about. Of course it can be achieved with a conductor, but it's really about developing a sense whose sophistication goes far beyond listening and reacting or watching and following. Even though this unanimity is the Holy Grail of ensemble singing it is remarkably easy to achieve. In adult education work with beginners I stop conducting at the earliest possible opportunity and witness people keying in to something that enables them to feel the music together; they listen to each other, they look at each other and a musical telepathy starts to develop. At the other end of the scale, with a professional choir, a passage can seem impossible to get together. If I stop conducting the ensemble will miraculously sort itself out. It's because the singers are trying harder and of course they're delighted to be demonstrating that they don't actually need me!

A characteristic of *O clap your hands* is that new sections often begin with a single part singing quite low in his or her register. The new words at these points must be heard clearly, so there needs to be a *diminuendo* in the first instance halfway through bar 7 to make way for Alto 1 in bar 8; and to provide contrast I suggest that "O sing unto God" is the start of a softer section. Tenor 2 will appreciate some help in bar 10; at speed those descending intervals will not be easy to tune.

I approach this music as I do the choral music of JS Bach. It's music of such extraordinary sophistication that a simple approach seems to work best, an approach that lets the music speak for itself; we began with a loud section, we followed that with a softer section and for the section starting in bar 17, "He is the great King", let's ask for *forte* until a *diminuendo* through bar 27 makes way for another softer section, begun again by Alto 1.

The challenge of contrapuntal music as distinct from melody and accompaniment is deciding what should be prominent at any given moment. In a Bach fugue we've often been told to bring out the subject. I liked the reaction of Francis Grier, my brilliant tutor at Oxford, to that instruction; he pointed out that Bach had sometimes gone to a great deal of trouble to hide the subject. Here, every voice has his or her moment and eventually everyone will know where those are and be able to enjoy his or her turn in the spotlight. As Bass 2 myself, I have a particular affection for bars 22 to 24. Of course, if it isn't your moment you need to make sure you are not giving too much.

We've got as far as adding *meno* in bar 28. After a chord change on virtually every beat, the idea of subduing the people is expressed by nearly three whole bars of one chord. The better in tune this is the more effective this moment will be. As described in the chapter on *The Evening Primrose*, start with the E flats, add the B flats and then slot in the Alto 2 G. If you decide that the dynamic should remain subdued until "He shall choose out an heritage for us" you had better encourage the singers to write *sempre piano*, otherwise it will get louder; contrapuntal writing can make choristers very competitive. The singers will naturally give more at the canonic section "He shall choose out an heritage for us" but the shaping needs to be elegant, particularly the octave leaps in Bass 1 and 2. A *decrescendo* through bars 42 and 43 can make way for a more *leggiero* approach to the entries of "ev'n the worship of Jacob" building up as every voice enters until the first part of the piece concludes *forte* at the double bar.

Attention to every single detail in polyphonic music is time consuming and unnecessary. We need to look at the big picture and, unlike their Tudor counterparts, modern choral singers have the advantage of looking at a score rather than just their own lines. I sometimes refer to the Palestrina principle. Looking at any page of a Mass or motet you'll notice that most of the notes are white and some of them are black. The likelihood is that the white ones are less interesting than the black ones. It's a gross simplification of course but at the very least a useful starting point. A cursory glance at a page of polyphony can reveal something unique in the texture which will get buried if we don't take care; Alto 2's three quavers/eighth-notes in bar 61 are unlike anything else, and even though they are low in the voice and everyone else is going hammer and tongs, I would love to give them a chance and fix the balance so that they can be heard.

After a *forte* start at "God is gone up" there are endless possibilities for the dynamics in the antiphonal "O sing praises". I note that I've well and truly broken my own punctuation rule in bar 64 and asked S1, A1 and T1 to sing through the full stop; I like the effect of doing that and starting "O sing praises" *piano*. Whatever you do dynamically the quavers/eighth-notes on "sing" and "o sing" will get lost if you don't find some length in them. I see this anthem as a series of musical panels each needing a dynamic approach appropriate to the words and distinct from what comes before and after. So, a *decrescendo* can prepare the ground for *legato forte* at "For God is the King of all the earth" in bar 80 followed by a gentler approach for "sing ye praises with the understanding". "God reigneth over the heathen" in bar 85 has a new and distinctive *sostenuto* quality and can be set up perfectly by everyone singing in bar 84 shortening his or her last note by a quaver/eighth-note and Tenor 2 being aware of what everyone else is doing. It's another test of the choir's unanimity. In bar 88 as previously, Alto 1 needs to be heard with the new idea so everyone else will need to make a *diminuendo*. Notice the rhythm on the Soprano 2 "heathen"; it's beautifully delicate and provides just a little more transparency for Alto 1. In the last verse of the Psalm Soprano 1 and 2 should enjoy the eccentricity of their rhythm at "doth defend the earth".

It may not be unique but I know of no other work where the Gloria dovetails as this one does in bar 105. Why doesn't Orlando Gibbons behave himself and bring the Psalm to a proper conclusion before starting the Gloria? Because he's a peerless, fearless, unfettered genius. It reminds me of the difficulty Beethoven seems to have in concluding some of his symphonies; he has created something of such energy and exuberance that it's very nearly unstoppable. There's a wealth of textural variety in the Gloria: a natural *diminuendo* as fewer and fewer voices sing in bars 114 to 118 is followed by the reverse effect in the next few bars. I'd like to be able to hear Bass 2 in bar 110 for its distinctive "Father" and my eye is drawn to Tenor 1 in the next two bars; it would be a shame not to be able to hear their version of "and to the Son". There are more decisions to be made in the closing bars but crucially it needs contrast, it mustn't get too loud too soon and there should always be a feeling of weightlessness.

How did it feel going back to an English anthem after Beethoven, Brahms, Verdi and Mendelssohn? For this former cathedral chorister it is summed up perfectly by T.S. Eliot:

> "We shall not cease from exploration
> And the end of all our exploring
> Will be to arrive where we started
> And know the place for the first time."

12

Rehearsing *At The Round Earth's Imagined Corners*, No.5 of *Songs of Farewell* by C. Hubert H. Parry

Born into a wealthy but tragic family, his mother died when he was twelve days old and three of his siblings had died in infancy, Hubert Parry's father's expectations would lead him first to a career in insurance with Lloyd's of London. But by his late twenties he had given that up in order to devote himself to music, initially working on the original *Dictionary of Music and Musicians* edited by George Grove. Comparison with his slightly younger contemporary Edward Elgar, in many ways, shows them as complete opposites: Elgar the Roman Catholic outsider and son of a piano tuner and Parry, educated at Eton and Oxford, destined to become Professor of Music at Oxford and Director of the Royal College of Music. Parry's reputation as a composer may not rival Elgar's, but as the composition teacher of Vaughan Williams, Holst and Frank Bridge who would become Britten's great mentor, he had played a key role in British music in the first half of the twentieth century and beyond by the time of his death, five weeks before the Armistice was signed ending the First World War.

Songs of Farewell is the work of a teacher, still Director of the Royal College of Music when he died, bidding farewell, not just to his own life, but to a generation of gifted young men, forced to abandon their South Kensington studies and take arms against their counterparts from the land of Bach, Beethoven and Wagner. An unimaginable weight of feelings could surely have imploded as he put pen to paper to set these five poems and finally a Psalm. Instead he produces, certainly in the case of this setting of one of Donne's *Holy Sonnets*, a part-song that compares favourably with any equivalent work by Elgar or Brahms, a work which looks back to the age of Orlando Gibbons without failing to notice the great Lieder composers on the way.

There's a way of getting exactly the right quality to this opening chord, a way we are very familiar with by now. A composer will often superfluously write a *crescendo* over an ascending phrase, but here the *crescendo* helps to create an immediate feeling of intensity, as does the opening rhythm sung in diminution by the lowest four voices. The accent on "earth's" can be achieved with or without a glottal; I would ask the upper four voices to do it without, and the lower three to do it with, so that something different is happening with the repetitions of the word, but care must be taken in the case of Tenor and Bass 1 who sing it together, that the word doesn't pop out of the texture. In this slow opening it's important of course to be slow, but not too slow, as you need to follow the *Allargando* marking in bar 9 and find a slower speed for the next section. It's also important not to be too loud too soon, and for details such as the Alto 1 triplets in bar 4 to have some presence; Soprano 1 can give themselves a chance to *crescendo* through the *Allargando* by by giving their accented *ff* entry a sense of *sforzando mf*. Most of the commas make sense as opportunities for breaths but it seems natural for Soprano 1, Alto 1, Tenor and Bass 2 to sing through theirs at the end of bar 8. Make sure the *staccato* in bar 9 is short but not accented. The little note in "and arise" always needs energy and surprisingly there is no *Allargando* in bar 15; the slower speed starts without warning on the *pp* chord. Bars 17 to 20 will benefit from separating melody from accompaniment and first rehearsing the quaver crotchet/eighth-note quarter-note motifs, making sure that they are in tune, together, and that they don't rush, before adding the melody lines whose fastidiously marked dynamics and accents perfectly capture the poet's Hieronymus Bosch-like vision of souls reuniting with their bodies. As long as it's discreet the d and t can be sounded in "and to" and I wouldn't subdivide before the last beat of bar 25.

Looking at the *Spiritoso* bars shows that when there's any sense of double-choir it's a case of high and low; the layout can reflect this with SATB reading from the conductor's left. Unlike Gibbons's *O clap your hands*, here the ranges of 1 and 2 are different. I refer you to the title of this book for the opening of the *Spiritoso* section; like the opening of William Walton's *Belshazzar's Feast* all the men are required to sing *forte* with accents, but intonation and quality need not be sacrificed. (Notice in bar 27 how Parry gives the top part to Bass 1 who are in a more potent part of their range than the tenors would be at these pitches.) Sounding both d's at "flood did" takes care of the accent. A pivotal moment in the poem and the motet provides one of its biggest challenges; I would use every possible device to engender confidence between bar 33, with its determined comma and tempo change halfway through, and the Alto 1 "And you whose eyes", for example getting Alto 1 to join Bass 1 in bar 33, but to sing the B they are going to need in the next bar on the last beat, sustaining it until their entry. Soprano 2 will benefit from devices too, for example stopping on and sustaining the octave C until it's really confident, and doing the same on the E, the B flat and the unison in bar 39. In fact, the whole of this section until the G major chords in bars 51 and 52 where the tenors and basses join, will benefit from the stop-and-sustain treatment. Breathing with the punctuation still works here with, for example, a breath for Soprano 2 and Alto 1 and 2 in bar 47.

Tenors and basses rejoin with a very special quality in bar 52, and the *tenuto* on every single note in the next bar is Parry insisting on *sostenuto* even though it's *ppp*. It's natural to sing through commas in almost every case here, though clearly there needs to be some separation between beats 1 and 2 in the accompanying voices in bar 54, throwing Alto 2 into as much relief as possible as they start their *crescendo* from *pp*. This singing through punctuation makes for long phrases, so breathing should be staggered but organised, avoiding any risk of holes. There needs to be a real sense of *legato* through the ascending fifth "me mourn" in bars 54 and 56 to 58. Soprano 2 can breathe after "space" in bar 57, but it needs to be after beat 3 in order to have a degree of subtlety before the extraordinary melisma on "mourn". In bar 60 Alto 1, Soprano 2 and Tenor can find expressive length in "and". It is this kind of *Lieder* singer detail that can elevate a choral performance to another level. The figure that everyone has in some form on "For, if above" needs care as the third note is short and, particularly in the case of Soprano 1, hard to tune. Parry marks *Agitato* for "'Tis late to ask abundance of thy grace". A middle way needs to be found here between its becoming too beautiful, even sentimental, and too hurried. It can be urgent without being too fast for all the detail to register; sounding both t's in "late to" will contribute to the right feel.

There's wonderfully inspired antiphonal writing at the start of the *Tranquillo* section. Though there appears to be no daylight before the restart in bar 72, there needs to be some silence after the Alto 1 resolution. The word "ground" must end with a perfectly tuned voiced d. This is one of the real tests of a choir; it will be most obvious in bar 78 where the minim/half-note can be shortened by a quaver/eighth-note, again providing a chink of light. Choral singers are very often reluctant to sing final voiced consonants and consequently ends of words can be wrong, "God" becomes "got", or they disappear altogether. To remedy this, I recommend elongating that final extra vowel until it's in tune, then shortening it and getting it absolutely rhythmic.

We are into the final section where time and care will be needed to nurse choristers through a few bars where enharmonic changes make the music look intimidating. (This is Parry looking back to the English Golden Age but catching sight of Schumann on the way.) There are plenty of common chords to stop on and sustain as previously. Parry identifies the lines that should be prominent using *tenuto* to signify *legato sostenuto* in bars 90 to 92 and finally in bar 101. Bars 94 to 96 don't have a line with *tenuto* markings, but *diminuendo* markings to *p* in other parts allow the tenors to shine with a new and special quality. In the final bars, a coda, because there was even more to be wrung from this last line of poetry, a *crescendo* towards the suspension on "pardon" might be instinctive but isn't written and should be resisted. I would not have made too much of the consonant clusters in "Thou'dst sealed" and "hadst sealed", and I'd be happy to let everybody elide the two th's in "with thy blood" until the basses have those words in the penultimate bar, when I would like to hear them both, with a subdivided last beat finding maximum weight in the upbeat to the last bar. "Blood", in bar 104 and the final bar, calls for an exquisite final voiced consonant.

Poetry of this quality does not usually attract composers; I don't believe Wilhelm Müller or Friedrich Rückert are rated as highly as John Donne. But the Baronet professor has taken on an expressionistic medieval vision of the Last Judgement, by the greatest of the metaphysical poets, and shown himself equal to it.

AT THE ROUND EARTH'S IMAGINED CORNERS

Words:
JOHN DONNE (1572-1631)

Music
C. HUBERT H. PARRY (1848-1918)

89
S.1
for that's as good As if Thou'dst sealed my par - - don,
S.2
that's as good As if Thou'dst sealed my par- don, as good
A.1
mf
for that's as good, as good As if Thou'dst sealed my
A.2
As if Thou'dst sealed my par don, as
T.
cresc.
mf
good, that's as good, as good As if Thou'dst sealed my par -
B.1
cresc.
mf
that's as good, as good, as good As
B.2
mf
as good, as good As
93
rit.
A tempo
p
poco cresc.
S.1
for that's as good as if Thou'dst sealed my par - don, as if Thou'dst sealed,
S.2
p
as if Thou'dst sealed my par - don, as if Thou'dst sealed, as
A.1
p
par - - - - - - don, as if Thou'dst sealed
A.2
p
cresc.
if Thou'dst sealed my par - don, as if Thou'dst sealed
T.
- don, as if Thou'dst sealed my par - - don,
B.1
if Thou'dst sealed my par - - - don,
B.2
if Thou'dst sealed my par - don hadst

97
rit.
S.1
— hadst sealed my par - - don with thy blood, as if Thou'dst sealed my
S.2
if Thou'dst sealed, hadst sealed my par - don, hadst sealed my
A.1
hadst sealed my par - - don with Thy blood, hadst sealed my
A.2
— my par - - - don with thy blood, hadst sealed my
T.
my par - don with Thy blood, hadst sealed my
B.1
as if Thou'dst sealed my par - don, hadst sealed my
B.2
sealed my par - don, sealed my
mf
p
102
rit. molto
S.1
par - don with Thy blood, as if Thou'dst sealed my par - don with thy blood.
S.2
par - don with Thy blood, as if Thou'dst sealed my par - don with thy blood.
A.1
par - don with Thy blood, as if Thou'dst sealed my par - don with thy blood.
A.2
par - don with Thy blood, as if Thou'dst sealed my par - don with thy blood.
T.
par - don with Thy blood, as if Thou'dst sealed my par - don with thy blood.
B.1
par - don with Thy blood, as if Thou'dst sealed my par - don with thy blood.
B.2
par - don with Thy blood, as if Thou'dst sealed my par - don with thy blood.
pp
ppp

13

Amen, Alleluja!

Although I had conducted choirs at school, at university and at The Royal College of Music, once I had left the RCM (where I had been studying singing for three years), I worked exclusively as a singer for the next twelve years. This was partly because what I had been learning about singing seemed far removed from the practice of choral conducting I had been brought up with, with its quasi-militaristic discipline and, in particular, what I now regarded as an overemphasis on consonants. If I had stood in front of a choir I could easily have found myself doing it in a way that no longer made sense. I wasn't ready. So I sang professionally, covering just about everything: more church music, opera and oratorio both as chorister and soloist, consort, close harmony and contemporary music. And having done this alongside a host of great colleagues and under some of the world's great conductors, but most importantly of all, having continued to study and receive coaching from some of the best in the business, I felt it was time at last for me to stand out front again with the benefit of all this experience. There was one major hurdle. I had to find a choir whose committee would take a risk with a singer who said he now wanted to conduct. It took two and a half years and I am eternally grateful to the committee of Cunninghame Choir in North Ayrshire for taking that risk with me; and in the Beith Community Centre on successive Wednesday evenings starting in September 2005 I brought my knowledge of singing to the task of choral conducting. The specifications of that choir will be familiar to many: there were between twenty and thirty singers, a shortage of young singers, a generous complement of altos, fewer sopranos and even fewer tenors. If you can't do the job under these circumstances you give the impression of not even being able to make a success of a community choir; but in fact, if I could do it here I decided, I could do it anywhere, and I distinctly remember the moment, working on the opening of the Gloria from the Beethoven *Mass in C*, when I realised it.

One of the discoveries of my two seasons with Cunninghame Choir was the transforming effect of finding length in every note, kneading pizza-dough rather than playing the xylophone, and that discovery was made principally in our preparation for a Rodgers and Hammerstein programme. The syllabic style of most of the music, almost always one note per syllable, makes it the perfect vehicle to demonstrate the benefits of the *legato sostenuto* approach. You need look no further than *My favorite things* to see what I mean. Do it wrong; no length, no quality. Then do it right, and feel the physicality of singing, once felt, never forgotten.

At music college the role of the singing teacher, who has taught you everything up to that point, divides into two. You are assigned your singing teacher who teaches technique, and assigned a coach, an accompanist, with whom you work on repertoire. So, if necessary your singing teacher can spend the whole lesson on the five vowels and posture; you have the opportunity to work on repertoire and get used to how it feels with the accompaniment with your coach. Robert Sutherland was one of the coaches at the RCM. He had the benefit of a lifetime's experience and had played for many great singers including Elisabeth Schwarzkopf and Maria Callas. Robert showed endless patience with me, in particular in getting me to realise that however similar they might look, the vocal line and the piano accompaniment in a Schubert or Schumann song could not be more different. *Abschied* from Schubert's *Schwanengesang* is a perfect example.

figure 5

The piano plays short notes but the singer sings long ones. Those black notes do look very similar, but they're not. The vocal line is an object lesson in *legato sostenuto*, the idea that would transform "Brown paper packages tied up with strings" and "Wild geese that fly with the moon on their wings" in the Beith Community Centre seventeen years later.

And these are a few of my favourite moments from the solo repertoire that can illuminate our approach to a thousand moments in the choral repertoire. If they have one thing in common it's a sense that the answer is in the least likely place.

As part of my preparation for the bass solo part in the Dvořák *Requiem Mass* I booked a session with Robert Sutherland. He will have helped me with every single bar but one moment stands out. Unlike other composers, Mozart, Verdi and Britten for example, Dvořák does not set the word "Lacrymosa" to any kind of tune.

figure 6

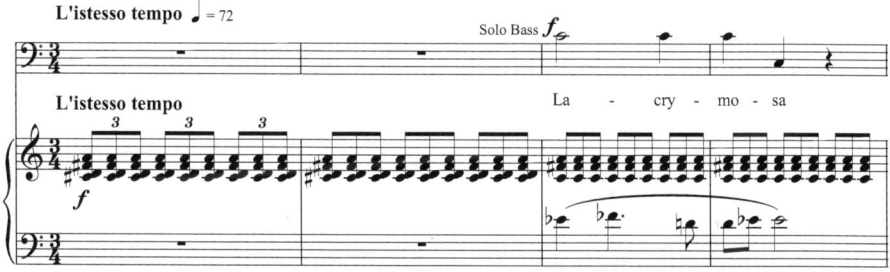

What can the bass soloist do with these rather unpromising four notes? Robert Sutherland had the answer. Find length in the "-cry-". It's the last beat of the bar and it's an unstressed syllable. Can the expressive potential of the word possibly be contained in that note? Yes, it can; the addition of a *tenuto* to that note brings the music to life and makes sense of how Dvořák has set the word. There weren't really any other possibilities; we've already learned to be cautious of big downbeats and there's very little left in this tiny phrase.

In her aria "Dich, teure Halle" from Wagner's *Tannhäuser*, Elisabeth needs to invest the words "geliebter Raum!" beloved room (the hall of song where she first saw Tannhäuser), with every drop of expressivity she can muster. See figure 7. Again it's an unstressed syllable that holds the key, not the down beat, not the middle syllable of "geliebter", where the stress falls in the spoken word, but the first of these four notes. She finds length in the "ge-" and the listener sits up.

figure 7

There are countless examples of this in English, German and Latin. Something wonderful happens when you find expressive potential by finding length in these upbeats. Look at "Ah! Belinda" from Purcell's *Dido and Aeneas* with that in mind, figure 8,

figure 8

and the last phrase from the first song of Schumann's *Dichterliebe*, figure 9; the juice is in the first syllable of "Verlangen".

figure 9

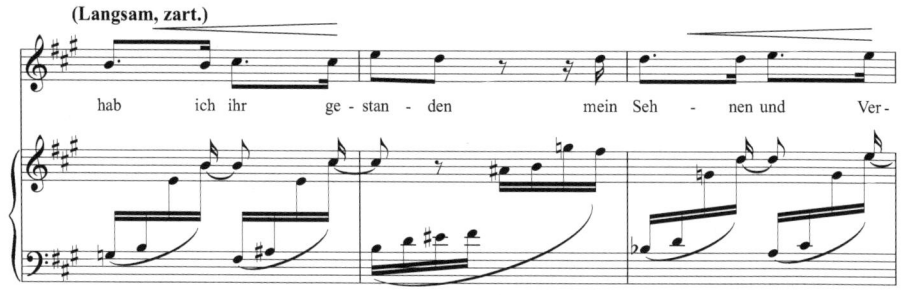

One more surprise, at least a revelation to countless oratorio students of mine. I have asked sopranos to sing the aria "With verdure clad" from Haydn's *The Creation*, figure 10, and then asked them what the most important word is in the phrase "By flowers sweet and gay". Some say "flowers", some say "sweet", and some say "gay". They proceed to sing it their way and my litmus paper stays resolutely blue. Then I ask them to find something special in the word "and". And the whole phrase is transformed.

figure 10

The big beats, the big words, the big ideas all speak for themselves. Find something to do with an ordinary word or a weak beat and you grab the listener's attention. He or she doesn't know why and if asked might start talking about an indefinable quality. That's fine. Don't spoil the illusion! But it's certainly not indefinable; we know exactly what we're doing. And bringing this knowledge from the one-to-one coaching session to the choral rehearsal, treating your choir like a room full of soloists, enables you to turn the water into wine again and again. It's a singer's approach to choral conducting.

Acknowledgements

No choral conductor is an island, and I am exceptionally fortunate in the teachers and colleagues, too numerous to name, from whom I continue to learn. My particular model singing teacher/choral director, with whom the idea of choral rehearsal as group singing lesson really started to crystallise, was Robert Dean of whom I would like to make special mention. I am grateful to Douglas Coombes for encouraging me to write the book in the first place and to Carole Lindsay-Douglas for immediately agreeing to publish it, for her belief in the project and enthusiasm and resourcefulness at every stage. I should like to thank my wife Clare for her encouragement particularly when reading the material for the first time, and for the expertise she was able to bring to the book's design, look and feel. Thanks too to my teenage daughter Talitha for demonstrating so beautifully every time she sings how important it is for youngsters to just do it, with only the vaguest notion that there might be such a thing as technique. Mitchell Sandler must be thanked for his eagle-eye for punctuation and for reassuring me that my ideas in print could easily be understood, as must the peerless musician/writer Andrew Gant for his careful consideration of the manuscript and his invaluable opinion that I was actually on to something very interesting.

EC Cromarty 2017

also from Lindsay Music

Chorus for Everyone
Bette Gray-Fow

Sound Singing
Gordon Pearce

Welcome to Choral Singing
Derek Harrison